Trouble
on the
Massacre

Trouble on the Massacre

Todhunter Ballard

WHEELER
CHIVERS

This Large Print edition is published by Wheeler Publishing, Waterville, Maine USA and by BBC Audiobooks Ltd, Bath, England.

Published in 2006 in the U.S. by arrangement with Golden West Literary Agency.

Published in 2006 in the U.K. by arrangement with Golden West Literary Agency.

U.S.   Softcover   1-59722-173-2 (Western)
U.K.   Hardcover   1-4056-3705-6 (Chivers Large Print)
U.K.   Softcover   1-4056-3706-4 (Camden Large Print)

Set in 16 pt. Plantin by Christina S. Huff.

Printed in the United States on permanent paper.

British Library Cataloguing-in-Publication Data available

Library of Congress Cataloging-in-Publication Data

Ballard, Todhunter, 1903–
    Trouble on the massacre / by Todhunter Ballard.
        p. cm. — (Wheeler Publishing large print westerns)
    ISBN 1-59722-173-2 (lg. print : sc : alk. paper)
    1. Large type books.   I. Title.   II. Wheeler large print western series.
PS3503. A5575T76 2006
813'.52—dc22   2005030649

Trouble on the Massacre

One

The horse had traveled a long way. So had the man. Both were gaunt, trail-streaked, and weary, and the camp they came to was hardly a camp at all, but just a little fire above the tumbling waters of the creek, set on a stony shelf where the sharp pitch of the canyon wall receded in a horseshoe and a small meadow widened the faint trail.

Young Boone Ralston heard them coming before they rounded the rocky shoulder above his fire, the downdraft telegraphing the sound of their travel. He straightened to frown into the surrounding darkness with quick nervousness. Then as the steady clink of shod hoofs on the higher trail continued, he hurried to his tethered horse, knowing that it could not be Ellen Jenner. She would come up-canyon, not down.

His impulse was to mount, to ride away before he could be seen, but he took a long breath to steady his shaky nerves, lifted the rifle from its boot beneath the saddle's fender and drifted away from the firelight into the screening night, retreating to the shelter of the aspens which grew down the canyon wall to the edge of the meadow.

He stopped then, turning to watch the trail, barely visible in the glare from the small fire. His rifle was ready as he saw the tired horse and man come slowly into view, the horse raising its drooping head and increasing its labored pace in hope that the camp marked an end to the struggle of its descent.

Boone saw the man straighten in the saddle, his figure seeming to grow taller as his shoulders came back and his chin rose. He checked the horse and sat motionless, then sent out his call, showing that he knew he was in a strange country and could observe the niceties of manners.

"Hello the fire." He sat, waiting an answer, and seemed more puzzled than alarmed by the lack of response. "Hello." He urged his horse forward into the circle of full light, not stepping down until the animal paused thankfully beside Boone Ralston's tethered roan.

Ralston came forward quietly. The stranger's back was toward him as the man held his hands to the warmth of the blaze, but when a branch snapped under

Ralston's foot the newcomer turned with the swiftness of an alert cat, his body slanted forward, his hand dropping by instinct to the butt of his holstered gun.

"Hold it." Boone Ralston's youthful voice cracked a little as he came into the circle of light. He stopped, trying to conceal his nervousness as he studied the man, the tense silence broken only by the giggle of the rapid creek as its waters tumbled over boulders that would block its course.

With relief he realized that the man was a total stranger. The face in the firelight showed lean under the mask of the week-old beard, as if its owner had missed more meals than he had taken. The eyes were grey-green, light, suggesting that they could flash fire if the man was aroused.

He stood for an instant, crouched, then straightened to his full six feet, bringing the hand slowly away from his gun, lifting it to raise his flat crowned hat and wipe his forehead with the sleeve of his sheep-lined coat.

His hair, thus exposed, was long, in need of cutting, a dark red, almost a sorrel in its brown overtones. He smiled then, as if he had found nothing to frighten him in Boone Ralston's set face.

"Spotted you from above. Wondered where you'd got to. I judge you don't much want company." As he said the last a trace of amusement touched the corner of his thin-lipped mouth, loosening it, seeming to soften the bony hardness of his face. He had already appraised the camp and, seeing no food and no spread blankets, had decided that this was not a night stop. "Is that right?" he asked, his voice mildly insistent.

Boone did not answer at once. He moved sidewise to a point from where he could see the brand burned on the flank of the stranger's horse. It was not a valley brand. In fact he had never seen it before and had no idea where it was registered.

The strange rider watched the movement. His lips tightened but he stood at ease, still keeping his hand clear of his gunbelt. Boone turned and came back, shifting his rifle, cradling it in the crook of his left arm.

"Where you from?"

The man gestured toward the white peaks which rose some twenty miles away, like a snag-toothed fence stretching into the arch of the star-filled sky. "Over the ridge."

Boone stared at him, incredulous. "No

one comes over the divide at this season of the year. The snow is thirty feet deep."

"I did." It was a simple statement, flat, allowing no argument.

Boone started to say something, then checked himself. What point was there, contradicting this drifter? "You must have had a good reason," he said.

"I did." The man's mouth quirked again, this time with a touch of self-mockery and something deeper. "I was in a hurry. It didn't seem wise to go around."

Boone Ralston studied him. He wished the man would ride on. He certainly wanted no witness to his meeting with Ellen Jenner. Time enough for the valley to learn of their alliance when they were ready to strike. But if the stranger continued on down the canyon now he was certain to meet the girl coming up. Better hold him here for a while and then ask him to avoid such a meeting.

He said, "Your business. Whatever you are running from must be powerful medicine. Hungry?"

The man smiled, this time wholeheartedly. "I could eat."

Boone walked back to his horse, replaced the rifle in its boot and got the sandwiches his sister had fixed for him from the saddlebag. "Sorry, I haven't any coffee."

"I have." The red-haired man went to his own animal and drew a blackened coffee pot from the slicker-wrapped roll behind the saddle. He filled the pot at the creek and placed it on the embers of the fire, throwing in a handful of coffee.

There had been a single battered cup within the pot. He placed it on a log and squatted on his heels, chewing on one of the cold beef sandwiches.

When the pot boiled he filled the cup and they took turns drinking the scalding black liquid. The canyon's downdraft beat against them, bringing with it the icy blasts from the snowfields above, but the warmth of the coffee caused the stranger to relax visibly. He expressed both weariness and gratification with a long, low groan of relief.

"I suppose you're wondering what I'm doing here," Boone Ralston said.

"I haven't asked."

"No," Boone said, "you haven't. I haven't asked your name either."

"It's Sanderson."

"What's in a name? You can call yourself Smith or Brown, or even Jones. I don't expect you to explain your actions to me."

Sanderson hid his smile. This boy talked younger than he looked, with a hint of bravado that sought to make an impression.

"You want a job?"

Sanderson considered, gazing at the fire, wondering what was in the boy's mind, who he was, and why he should offer work to a chance stranger. "I think not," he said finally.

Boone Ralston was disappointed. He had sized Sanderson up: the way he wore his gun, the way he carried himself, the watchful attention he gave to each small detail without appearing to be nervous. To him it all added up to one thing — an outlaw, a man riding away from something. Why else would anyone cross the ridge at this season of the year? Only a fool or a greenhorn would try it, and certainly this Sanderson was neither.

"We'd pay well," he said.

"Who are we?"

Ralston recaptured the caution he had forgotten for the moment. "Oh, some friends of mine. They're putting on new hands."

"Sorry. I hadn't planned to stay in the country long."

The boy considered. They needed men desperately. Maybe Ellen could talk Sanderson into joining them, but could they trust him? Might he not change sides once he understood the situation in the valley? Better to let him go than expose their plans to a stranger.

He said with an attempt at frankness, "I never explain my actions to anyone, but in this case I'm going to. I'm here to meet a girl. It may seem a strange place for it, but believe me, friend, I have very good reasons for picking this spot."

"So?" Sanderson continued to be amused. The boy took himself so seriously.

"So when we hear her coming, which should be in a very few minutes, I have a favor to ask. I'd like you to take your horse and circle back across this meadow to the timber. You can follow its edge down and come back to the trail a hundred feet below. If you're careful the wind and the noise of the creek will cover your going and she won't know anyone else was here."

Sanderson laughed. "Afraid that sight of me might scare her?"

"It isn't that." Ralston was very intent. "She insisted that I tell no one of our meeting. I wouldn't want her to think I broke my word. This is our private business, you see. I judge that you aren't a man who likes strangers interfering in his private affairs and therefore you wouldn't want to interfere in ours."

"That seems fair enough. What's the closest town, and how do I get there?"

"The town is Massacre. You drop out of this canyon and follow the trail until you strike a main road. Turn left into the road. The town will be about five miles away."

"An odd name, Massacre."

Ralston's smile was bitter. "Not odd, when you know the valley and its history. The town is named for the creek." He indicated the swift water with a motion of his hand. "So is the valley below us. The story is that a band of half starved Indians were slaughtered here in this canyon by as stupid a glory hunter as ever wore the uniform. There was one Indian left and he put a curse on the valley. I don't know about most curses, but this one seemed to work. Eleven people have been killed down there in the last few years."

Sanderson did not answer. He had heard sound from the canyon below them. He rose, freed his horse without speaking and led it into the darkness of the meadow, heading for the timber line.

Just before he faded from the tiny circle of firelight he raised his hand in a kind of salute, thanks and farewell, and he called softly, "Good luck."

Boone Ralston did not answer. He did not expect to see the tall man again. He turned, looking down trail, waiting for the girl to appear.

Sanderson reached the timber before she rode up and dismounted. He found the mouth of a small side canyon and worked the horse into it, completely screened from the fire two hundred feet away. There he tied the animal, knowing that it was too weary even to search for food, and came back to the edge of the trees to settle himself on the hard ground, his back against the bole of an aspen, his coat collar raised against the downdraft, his eyes on the figures of Boone and the girl which were little more than silhouettes between him and the faint glow of the dying fire.

The noise of the stream and the wind, and the distance, muted their voices until he could hear no word that was said, but he watched them intently, not with idle curiosity but because the meeting puzzled him. The offer of a job, the boy's manner and now the actions of the two beside the fire whispered more of conspiracy than of a lovers' tryst.

They talked for nearly half an hour. Had

they kissed at parting, or even clasped hands, he might have revised his thinking, but the girl simply turned and walked to her horse, mounted and rode down canyon without even waving goodby.

Boone Ralston watched her, then went slowly to kick the fire apart and douse it with water from the coffee pot which Sanderson had deliberately forgotten. Afterwards the boy lifted himself into the saddle and headed down-trail, following the girl, the clink of his horse's shoes on the rocks dying to nothingness as he rounded the lower bend.

Still Sanderson did not move. He sat quiet, wrapped in his sheep-lined coat, listening to the wind and the water. He sat thus for a good half-hour, until he was certain they had cleared the canyon mouth. Then he found his horse, untied it and led it back to the trail, mounting and letting it pick its careful way down the stony track until they came out with amazing suddenness on the bench of the wide valley.

Here the moon which had been masked out by the trees on the canyon wall rode high in the eastern sky, throwing the country below Sanderson into sharp relief, the high bench on which he sat, the trail zigzagging downward to the grass cushion of the valley floor and the second range far to the east, where snow glistened whitely on the harsh upthrusts of the enormous peaks.

He urged the horse forward, dropping down the loops of twisting trail until it smudged out in the rutted wagon tracks of a well traveled road which slanted north and south following the axis of the main valley.

He paused again, then turned left into the road as Boone Ralston had directed. He rode up the rising grade of a small hill and reached the crest just in time to meet a heavy freight wagon that had come up the opposite slope.

The teamster pulled in to let his four mules blow and Sanderson's horse halted beside the wagon without direction from the rider. The man in the wagon was bearded, bundled against the chill, his nose red and dripping under the shadow of his broken hat.

"Cold night," he said.

Sanderson nodded. He used the pause to draw out his tobacco and shake the fine grains into the cupped paper. The teamster watched with a kind of hunger and Sanderson extended the small cloth sack across the high front wheel.

"How far to Massacre?"

The man was busy licking the cigarette. When he finished he said, "Ten thousand miles maybe if you keep headed the way you're going. You're riding in the wrong direction."

Sanderson held a match sheltered in his hands for the other light. He was certain he had not misunderstood the directions. He had been told to turn left when he reached the road.

Either Boone Ralston had not wanted him to reach Massacre, or this was the boy's idea of a joke. "How far to the next town this way?" He pointed in the direction the teamster had come from.

"Fifty-five miles."

"Thanks," he said. "My horse would never make it." He pulled the animal around and rode back down the hill he had just climbed.

Two

The town did not impress Sanderson. It sprawled beside the creek, where the stream widened out and slowed its pace and looped through flat, grassy meadows, sedate as a mill pond as if trying to atone for the wild force with which it had rushed out of the canyon only ten miles to the north.

There were four streets, rutted and dusty, for the valley had had no rain in three weeks, and beyond the even rows of lumber and log buildings which bordered the roadways, a hundred shacks stood canted at crazy angles as if their builders had purposely tried to express a dislike of regimentation by building as they chose without regard to what their neighbors had done. These shacks were reached by paths or tracks which could not be called streets in any sense of the word.

Sanderson walked his horse down the main thorofare until he came to a weathered building whose fading sign read,

POPE'S LIVERY, and turned the tired animal into the covered runway.

He had hardly stepped from the saddle when the hostler appeared from the lantern-lit office. The man was old and thin, and his nutcracker jaws showed plainly that he had few teeth behind his sunken cheeks. "Putting up?"

Sanderson nodded. He stretched, trying to take the kinks out of his tired muscles, and pulled the hunting case watch from his vest pocket. He was surprised to find that it was only nine thirty.

He loosened the bedroll from behind the saddle, pulled his carbine from the boot, loosened the double cinch and swung the heavy saddle to the rack beside the front box stall.

"Place to sleep in town?" he asked the hostler.

"Uh-huh. Hotel two blocks down the street."

"Any good?"

The toothless one shrugged. "I sleep here."

Sanderson debated. It would not be the first barn he had slept in, but it was a full two weeks since he had started over the mountains, and in that time he had had neither a bath nor a bed.

"I'll try the hotel." He left his carbine in the barn office, hefted the blanket roll, swinging it to his shoulder, and moved up the main street. He passed three saloons before he reached the corner on which the hotel stood.

The hotel seemed to be the only two-storied structure in Massacre. Built of hand-squared logs chinked with a white mud, it boasted a narrow gallery and two big front windows.

He climbed the two steps to the gallery, crossed it and came into a long, narrow lobby lighted by a single swinging lamp which dangled on its chains from the long center beam.

The beam, squared as were the logs of the outer walls, was sixty feet in length, with deep adze marks showing on its rough faces. Just inside the front door Sanderson paused to look around the room, noting the cane bottomed chairs lined along the wall, the board floor, scarred by a thousand spurs, the high desk at the rear in the shadow of the open stairway.

It seemed to him that the same man must have built all cow country hotels. Some were better than others, clean and well run, but there was a sameness in their architectural arrangement, as unvarying as the quality of food most of them served.

A hand bell on the corner of the high desk bore a small printed card: Ring for Service. He tapped it and waited. A large fleshy woman came from the dark dining room and looked at him with a measuring gaze as she wedged herself behind the desk.

Her eyes were a protruding brown in the heaviness of her reddish face, her dress was faded from too many washings and the skin of her arms, bare to the elbow, pouched and hung as if her hide had stretched more than the rest of her.

"A room," he said. "I suppose it's too late to get any hot water."

Her face showed her discontent with life and her voice had a raw complaining sound. "The reservoir may still be warm. I ain't promising a thing." She turned the ruled notebook which did for a register.

As he wrote his name he scanned the half page of smeared signatures above his and failed to find the one he sought. This was no surprise. Craig would probably have avoided a hotel. He might not even have come to Massacre, but turned the other way when he reached the road. Or he might have continued eastward across the valley toward the next mountain range.

Sanderson knew a feeling of deep discouragement. It had been easy enough to find marks of the man's passage in the mountains, but once out of the canyon, the trail was probably lost.

The woman noted his interest in the ledger. Ten years of running frontier hotels had sharpened her senses. She looked at his name, at the slanting script, bold yet without flourish — *James J. Sanderson* — and saw that he had not written an address below it. Still she held her comment, turning to the open key rack and handing down a brass tabbed key.

"A dollar in advance," she said.

He paid the dollar and waited beside the desk until she brought hot water in a battered tin pitcher. Then he climbed the stairs and went along the upper hall, lighted by a single lamp in a wall bracket, and found his room, the last one on the right.

Lifeless air greeted him as the door came open. The room smelled as if it had not been aired since the preceding winter. He set the pitcher on the floor, struck a match, found the lamp and lighted it, then moved to the shadeless window to look down at the alley which ran behind the hotel.

Below him, a shed roof which he judged covered the kitchen ran downward at a thirty degree angle, its metal sheeting gleaming dully in the moonlight.

Turning back, he shucked the trail-caked clothes from his tired body. Then he unfastened the bedroll, fished out his razor and scraped the two-week beard from his lean cheeks. Snow water and lack of soap made shaving on the trail impossible.

After that he bathed, standing on the ragged bit of braided rug over the splintered floor. The water in the bowl was barely tepid now, but along with the grime it washed some of the fatigue out of his long muscles.

He dressed, feeling ten years younger, alert and suddenly wolfishly hungry. The sandwich the boy had given him in the canyon was all the food he had eaten that day.

He stowed his gear in the battered bureau. It was an act he had repeated a hundred times in different towns, in other hotels, so that already the cell-like room, the scarred wallpaper, and the sagging bed had become his home.

Running the comb through his shaggy

hair he grimaced at his reflection in the wavy mirror, wondering how long the search would last, where the trail would end.

Craig might well be a hundred miles from Massacre by now, still riding hard. But no matter where he went, or how he tried to hide, Sanderson meant to find him. This was one search he would not abandon as long as he had life and strength to follow. That made it different from any other manhunt he had ridden upon. This was more than a job; this was a personal thing.

A knock at the door startled him. By instinct he moved toward the gunbelt and heavy weapon lying on the bed. Then, with a slight shrug and still holding the comb, he called, "Come in."

The door swung inward to reveal a man of middle age. He was thick of body, chunky and solid. His hair, neatly combed to give him almost a dandy's look, was already thin and its fringes showed traces of grey which matched his eyes. As light as shadowed snow, those eyes caught and held Sanderson's attention. Long ago he had learned to judge eyes, and in all of his experience he had known only a single killer whose eyes were brown.

"Come in," he said, openly watchful, and the man closed the door and moved solidly into the room's narrow confines. There was a wariness about the newcomer, an alertness, put there by aptitude and training and long habit. It marked him as he took three steps forward. He stopped, measuring Sanderson as if he wanted to make certain that he would recognize him again.

"Stranger in the valley?"

Sanderson laid the comb on the bureau. He had been standing half quartered to the stocky man. He turned to face his visitor, his long body slack, as if no tension touched him.

"That's right."

"Business in Massacre?"

Sanderson's thin lips quirked, but the smile did not quite touch his eyes. "I never heard of the town until two hours ago."

"Just passing through?"

Sanderson appeared to consider the question with a great deal more care than it deserved. "We'll see."

The visitor's grey eyes darkened. "That's not much of an answer," he said.

Sanderson's voice was soft, very low. "It wasn't much of a question, now that I think of it. I'm sorry but I don't quite understand your right to question me."

"I'm marshal here." The way he said it, with a trace of pompousness which did not quite fit him, made Sanderson curious.

"And as marshal, do you always question every stranger who happens to ride into Massacre?"

Suddenly Sanderson realized that the chunky man was uncomfortable. Not because of fear. He had lived through too many tight situations not to sense when someone was afraid. He guessed that the pomposity might have been caused by embarrassment.

"No, but my wife noticed how you examined the ledger when you registered, as if you were looking for a certain name. Who are you after?"

Sanderson had the picture now — the woman downstairs spotting his curiosity, going back to the kitchen, forcing her unwilling husband to come up here and ask questions.

It told him much about the man, and the woman who ran the hotel, and for that matter perhaps certain things about the town. Every community had its own peculiarities, colored by the character of the people who lived within its borders. Towns might look alike as to buildings and streets and dust, but here the similarity usually ended.

He said, easily, "Anything wrong with looking at your register? It's a habit of mine, every new town I hit. I might meet an old friend."

The marshal did not believe him. It showed in his light eyes. And he was not a fool, even if on occasion he took orders from his wife. He said solidly, "We have enough trouble in this valley without borrowing from outside."

"So I've heard." They looked at each other, if not with liking, at least with respect, for each realized that the other man had admirable qualities. "Is it too late to get something to eat?"

The marshal was glad to change the subject. "It's too late here. The stove is out and Hannah wouldn't fire it up again for the devil himself." He smiled thinly. "I'd rather go hungry than ask her."

"Anywhere else that might be open?"

"Mary Ralston is probably still at her place. It's a block north on the other side of the street."

Sanderson nodded. "Thanks." It was dismissal, but now the marshal did not quite know what to do. He was angry, not with Sanderson but with himself for allowing his wife to send him on the fool's errand.

Once again he realized that she was not nearly as good a judge of human nature as she thought.

She had said, "A saddle tramp just rented a room. He hasn't shaved for days and his clothes aren't fit for a rummage sale. He's looking for someone and I can smell trouble. Better tell him to leave town before he starts something."

Sanderson was not a saddle tramp. Bert Oxford had spent too many years policing cow towns not to spot the breed at once. He could sense the man's certainness of purpose. Without being able to classify Sanderson, he knew the man had not ridden into Massacre by accident.

What did the man want? Was he running from something, or running after something? Either way, it had to be a personal matter. Had he been a law officer his natural move would have been to introduce himself to the marshal.

He said a little lamely, "I hope you find something to eat, and keep out of trouble. We run a quiet town." He turned then and went out, shutting the door softly behind him.

Sanderson stared at the flimsy panel, then slowly picked up his gunbelt and fastened it around the flatness of his hips. Afterward he slipped into his heavy coat and left the room.

It was the first of May but in the high country the spice of winter still lingered in the air. It would be the Fourth of July before the drifts in the upper canyons faded under the onslaught of the summer sun.

As he came out onto the dark street he breathed deeply, the thin air stinging his nose with its coldness, a welcome relief after the stuffy room.

He had spent at least half of his adult years out of doors and no matter how elaborate the room he found it confining after a while. He crossed the street and moved along the dark store windows to the restaurant. The outer door was locked, but a light still burned in the kitchen at the rear. He knocked loudly.

Through the glass upper panel of the door he saw a slender, dark haired girl, slight in her grey dress as she swept across the dining room illuminated only by the reflection from the kitchen.

She paused, peering at him through the pane, and he knew that he was little more than a shadow between her and the moon-lighted street.

"We're closed. Who is it, please?"

Her voice came clearly through the glass, warm, a little husky; she spoke deep in her throat, almost like a man.

"A stranger," he said. "My name is Sanderson. I just rode in a little while ago. They told me at the hotel I might get something to eat here."

"We're closed." She repeated the words, but she did not turn away from the door.

"Is there any place else in town I can get food? I haven't had a real meal in several days."

She shook her head. She seemed to be considering; then as if against her better judgment she reached down, slid back the bolt and pulled open the door.

Warm air came out to greet him, air mingled with the teasing odors of coffee and cooked meat and herbs. Until that moment he had not known how utterly ravenous he was.

"Come in."

She stepped backward and he followed her, closing the door, conscious that she was measuring him speculatively in the half light of the room.

"I can give you some bacon and eggs."

He swallowed saliva. "That will be fine. About half a dozen eggs. And if you have some potatoes or cold beans —"

"I have boiled potatoes I could fry."

He said fervently, "You are an angel, ma'am. You see here the hungriest man in Colorado."

She smiled then, and it loosened the dark prettiness of her face and made her beautiful, bringing it alive with a warmth he had seldom seen.

"You sound really hungry."

"You have never seen a man so nearly dead of starvation who is still on his feet."

She led the way into the kitchen. The place was scrubbed, the pine board walls gleaming white in the lamplight.

He sat at the plain table, suddenly relaxed, feeling more at home than he could recall feeling in all the years since he had left his mother's house, and watched the girl's deft movements as she worked around the big stove.

Curiosity tugged at him. What was she doing here, who was she? Why was a girl as handsome as this not married?

"Do you run this place all alone?" he asked.

She nodded without turning.

"Your family live in Massacre?"

"My brother does."

He remembered suddenly the name the marshal had used — Mary Ralston — and said slowly, "Your brother, would his first name be Boone?"

This time she came around, her eyes showing surprise. "Why, yes. Do you know him?"

He said carefully, "I met him a little while ago," and said no more. He did not tell her about the fire in the canyon, or the girl who had ridden up there to meet the boy, but his curiosity increased a hundredfold.

She set the heaped plate before him. He ate slowly yet with full enjoyment, until the last bite was gone. Then he drank the coffee slowly.

"You were hungry." She had taken the chair across from him. "I never saw anyone put away as much."

He pushed back his chair. "I came over the ridge. I didn't have much food with me and very little chance to cook."

"Over the ridge?" Her eyelashes fluttered. "But how, at this season of the year?"

"I had little choice."

She had drawn away, pulling back into herself. Her manner until that moment had been as natural as if they were old friends. He could guess what she was thinking and he hated to deceive her, but it would be better if this town believed he was running from something until he found the man he sought.

He rose, regretting that she would share this doubt of him. Not that it really mattered, of course. The chances were many that he would not see her again.

"That was almost the best meal I can remember."

"Hunger," she said, "is a sauce that turns the plainest fare into a banquet."

"How much?"

She hesitated and a faint smile returned to her dark eyes. "The order is not a usual one."

He laid two dollars on the scrubbed table. "Enough?"

"It's far too much. I —"

"Your prices should go up after closing hours." He returned her smile and picked up his hat from where he had placed it and moved out into the semi-darkness of the dining room, conscious that she followed him.

At the door he drew the bolt and turned. "Thank you again for saving a starving man. Good night."

"Goodbye." Her tone was final. Plainly she did not expect to see him again.

Three

The Bearpaw Saloon was a long room smelling of wood smoke and spilled liquor and human sweat. Sanderson came into the warmth from the cold of the street to find half a dozen men scattered along the worn bar, five playing poker at a table in the rear, and Boone Ralston alone at another table against the back wall.

From long habit he paused just inside the door to examine the room for possible danger. The men at the bar glanced around and he saw the curiosity in their bearded faces before they returned to their drinks.

Only the card players and Ralston showed no interest in his arrival. He had meant to have a single drink and return to the hotel, but sudden impulse made him walk back past the bar, around the card game, to where Ralston sat alone.

He did not try to analyze the impulse, but he knew it had little to do with the boy. Rather, it involved the girl he had just left at the restaurant and his desire to know more about her.

Ralston sat with his shoulders hunched, elbows on the cloth covering, hands cupped around a glass into which he stared unseeing as if his thoughts were miles away.

"Mind if I sit down?" Jim Sanderson said.

The boy looked up with a visible start. His dark eyes were very like those of his sister.

"You?" There was surprise in the tone, and something else, something akin to fear.

Sanderson pulled out a chair and sat down. "Didn't you expect to see me? You told me how to get to Massacre."

Boone Ralston raised the glass he had been nursing between his hands and drained it at a single gulp. He returned it to the table slowly, plainly playing for time. Finally he said in a tight voice, "You know I didn't. You know I told you to take the left turn into the road. I thought you'd be in Fairview by morning."

"Why?"

"What difference does it make?" Boone's rather handsome face was sullen, but the resemblance to his sister was very strong.

Sanderson decided that the boy was the younger of the two. Although it hadn't been too apparent in the uncertain firelight in the canyon, immaturity showed now in Boone Ralston's pouting mouth, in the resentment behind his eyes, in a kind of brash rebellion.

Sanderson's voice tightened and his light eyes were bleak. "It makes the difference to me that my horse would never have reached Fairview. He was about finished. Do you usually make a joke of giving wrong directions to strangers?"

The boy tried to bluster. "I have a right to do anything I please."

"Do you?" Sanderson said. "What you need is a piece of strap across your back. You still aren't too big to whip."

Mild temper flared in Boone Ralston. "Try it," he said.

Sanderson had no intention of trying it. Not that he doubted his ability to whip the kid but teaching Ralston a lesson wasn't his affair.

He said "What did you hope to gain by sending me the wrong way?"

For a moment it seemed that Ralston would not answer. He shoved back his chair and started to rise. Then he changed his mind and leaned forward.

38

"All right. I'll tell you why I tried to keep you from riding into Massacre. I was trying to protect someone."

"Protect — who? The girl in the canyon?"

Ralston nodded.

"What made you think she had anything to fear from me?"

The boy edged his chair forward again. "From you, nothing directly. But if you happened to mention that I met her in the hills there are people who would guess who she was and what we're up to."

"Well?"

"So I'm going to ask you to promise not to mention our meeting in the canyon to anyone."

Sanderson's straight lips curved a little. "There's hardly a soul in this town I know well enough to pass the time of day with. I wouldn't recognize your friend if I met her on the street. I don't know what you and she are planning and I have no interest in it. I have problems of my own."

Ralston sat back, relief slackening his frown. "Thank you. I'm sorry I directed you wrong, but I was trying to play safe. Let me buy a drink." He raised his hand, motioning to the distant bartender. "Bring a bottle and another glass, Snyder."

The bartender was a fat man whose

moonlike face was spoiled by his nose, overlarge, out of place and laced with red veins turning purple. He came around the end of the bar carrying a bottle and a glass. He set them before Sanderson, but he addressed Boone Ralston.

"Your friend can drink," he said. "You've had enough."

Ralston flushed, and he tried to make his voice hard. He succeeded merely in making it climb an octave. "What's the matter with you, Snyder?"

The bartender was not impressed. "You were in here drinking this afternoon, and you've had four since you came back. Go home and sleep it off."

"Now you listen to me, Snyder Hawks. No one tells me —"

"You listen." Sanderson got the impression that in spite of the fat the bartender was not a soft man. "I serve any man I choose. And I don't choose to serve you. I'm not going to have your sister raising hell because her baby brother got drunk in my place. You should be ashamed of yourself, sitting around letting her work to support you."

Ralston's voice quivered with injured pride. "There are other places in town a man can drink, Snyder."

"Go to them then. You'll get no more here tonight."

The boy slammed his chair back against the wall and lunged to his feet. "Come on, Sanderson, this place stinks."

Sanderson knew that the bartender was watching him from the corner of his eye, ready for trouble. He said calmly, "Keep your hair on. This is the first drink I've seen in days. I'll not leave until it's finished."

He saw the smile form on the bartender's fat face, saw the man turn away toward the bar. Ralston stood undecided, not knowing quite what to do. Slowly he settled back into his place, his face brooding. There was, Sanderson realized, something deeper here than the mere refusal of a drink. The fat man had registered a lot of disapproval when he rebuked Ralston for sitting by and letting his sister support him.

But Sanderson had almost no time to think about it. The street door behind him banged inward and he turned his head in time to see four men appear.

Ralston saw them too, and his whole manner altered in a single breath. He leaned forward, his hands palm flat on the table's top, his mouth open as if he had been about to speak and then lost the urge.

Presently his tongue came out, its red tip circling his lips, moistening them. Behind Sanderson, the conversation at the bar halted in mid-word, and in the quiet he heard the scuff of the newcomers' boots as they tramped back past the poker game.

He knew with a kind of instinct that they were headed for his table. He had sensed it even as they came through the front door, but a glance at Ralston told him that the men were after the boy, not after him.

All the anger had washed out of the boy's face and fear replaced it. The dark eyes flicked this way and that, searching a means of escape.

The footsteps stopped behind Sanderson. He could not see the men without turning, and he did not turn. He sensed that any motion would bring on sharp, quick-breaking action.

They stood, not speaking, not moving, for a long minute, their heavy breathing the only sign of their presence. Then one of them came to the table on Sanderson's right.

He was a big man, with powerful shoulders under his heavy coat, a handsome man, self-assured, almost regal in his bearing. He ignored Sanderson, staring at Ralston as a snake stares at a chicken, and his silence carried a threat more plain than words. Then he turned his head and measured Sanderson as he might have examined a horse.

"Who are you?"

Sanderson had poured but not yet tasted his whiskey. Deliberately he picked up the small glass, raised it to his lips and drank it slowly.

He resented the man's manner, but he was too skilled a hand to allow himself to be goaded by words into something he did not understand and for which he was not ready.

"I asked you a question." The man's bearded jaw jutted at him.

"I heard you," Sanderson said.

"Then answer."

Sanderson shoved back his chair and rose leisurely. He kept his motions measured so that no abrupt action on his part would send the men into sudden action.

"The name," he said evenly, "is Sanderson."

"What are you doing in Massacre?"

"Riding through." He was having increasing difficulty holding his voice quiet. This bulky man irritated him with both tone and manner.

The man inspected him arrogantly. "A

saddle tramp." He said it with all the contempt that settled ranchers felt for the wandering breed. "All right. Get your horse and move on. Get out of this valley as fast as you can. I suppose this kid offered you a job. Don't take it."

Sanderson had a glimpse of Ralston's face. At the mention of a job he saw despair flare in the eyes and then a growing resolution, the resolution of an animal which realizes that it is cornered and will have to fight.

The words had a choked sound as he brought them out painfully. "You don't own this valley, Stover."

"We'll see who owns it." Stover sneered. "You and Ellen Jenner have big plans. Don't think you caught us asleep, Boone. You've been warned before, and you wouldn't listen. All right. You'll listen now."

He reached across the table and his big hand caught the front of Ralston's shirt. He jerked the boy forward across the edge of the table and with his other hand lifted Ralston's gun from the holster before Ralston could stop him. Then he slashed it down in a murderous arc along the side of Boone's head.

The boy sagged and would have fallen

save for the restraining hand still clutching his shirt.

"That's enough," Sanderson said.

Stover struck again, the gun barrel breaking the skin above Boone's temple. Sanderson hit Stover hard, in the side, under the extended arm which held the boy. The blow knocked the wind out of the big man. His grip relaxed and Boone went forward, striking his face on the table top, lying senseless and inert, half on, half off of the table.

Stover grabbed at the back of a chair to steady himself. With his other hand he brought up Ralston's gun, intending to shoot Sanderson. Sanderson scooped up the whiskey bottle and threw it. The bottle struck Stover's nose across the high bridge, breaking the cartilage with an audible crunch.

Reaction tightened the man's trigger finger and the gun exploded, the slug digging into the rough floor between Sanderson's feet. But there was no second shot. Sanderson grabbed Stover's gun wrist with one hand, twisting it viciously until the weapon clattered to the splintered floor, and at the same moment he buried his free fist in the man's face, further smashing the already shattered nose.

Blindly Stover tried to pull his wrist free and failed to break the grip of Sanderson's fingers. Sanderson twisted, using his hip, levering the arm across it, bending it backward until the bone snapped.

The hoarse cry of pain which burst from Stover was like a bugle call to his three followers. The action had been so swift it had caught them unprepared and they had stood frozen, unable to move during the seconds it took Sanderson to dispose of their foreman.

Now they charged, one jumping on Sanderson's back, the others trying to knock his legs from under him. The four went down together, and their very number helped defeat their purpose. One straddled Sanderson's back, trying to pin him to the floor while the others beat at his head, but it didn't work.

Sanderson heaved suddenly, lifting himself like a sunfishing horse, and threw the man from his back over his head to crash against Stover who had been just standing nursing his broken arm.

Those two went down in a tangle as the remaining two riders grabbed Sanderson, trying to wrestle him again to the floor. He was too strong for them, and he had years of training in rough and tumble fighting.

He got his powerful legs under him and came up, bringing them with him, and the violence which lurked in his big body exploded like a cyclone, gathering power and ferocity.

He shook them free like a dog shedding water after falling in the creek. One dropped to his knees and pawed with his hand at his holstered gun. Sanderson kicked him squarely under the chin, lifting the head until it threatened to snap from the neck as he went over backwards and lay quiet, cold as if he had been hit with a club.

His fellow scrambled away like a frightened crab. He made his feet and turned, starting to run, but Sanderson reached him in three panther leaps, caught him up by the collar and one leg and flung the body half across the room to crash into the hot stove.

It toppled from its base, spilling burning coals across the uneven floor. Jim Sanderson pivoted as the man he had hurled against Stover charged. He caught him by the throat, lifted him with one hand, holding him clear of the floor, shaking him as a terrier shakes a rat. The man's face went red, then purple from lack of air. Sanderson released his grip and the man dropped, collapsing on the floor limp as a sack of meal.

Sanderson stepped across him to face Stover. "Had enough?"

Stover gurgled incoherently. Rage, pain and hate clogged his throat, making it hard for him to speak. Dred Stover was used to having his own way. He had a bully's instincts and a native arrogance which made it hard for him to bow to any man. But as he met the grey green eyes he was suddenly afraid, and the knowledge that he was afraid only increased his hate.

"You'll never live to get out of this valley," he said in a hoarse whisper.

Sanderson's upper lip was rubbed raw where his face had been shoved against the floor, but it twisted in a mocking smile. "Keep talking," he said, "and you won't live to leave this room." He took a step and his hand snaked out, lifting Stover's gun, tossing it toward the far wall. It narrowly missed the fat bartender who had rushed from his place to slosh a bucket of water on the already smoldering boards where the stove had scattered ashes.

Everyone in the saloon was motionless, watching Sanderson, wondering what he would do next.

He backed away from Stover, stealing a

glance toward Boone Ralston. The boy had pushed himself erect. He stood beyond the table, dazed, blood running down from the broken skin above his temple.

Sanderson's attention came back to Stover and his three men, who were coming slowly to their feet. Dred Stover's eyes met Sanderson's, still angry, but he now had the anger under control. He grumbled an order and his men moved toward the door. He followed them, still nursing the broken arm with his good hand.

The door slammed. The bartender kicked at the damp ashes beside the overturned stove, then stooped and lifted it back into position, reassured that the danger of fire had passed.

He came to where Sanderson stood.

"I wouldn't have believed it," he said.

"What wouldn't you have believed?" Sanderson said.

"That one man, any man, could lick Dred Stover and three of his riders. No sir. Nothing like that has happened in this valley for years and years. Stover runs the place. You did a nice job, mister, but if you're smart you'll mount your horse and ride out. Stover is licked tonight, but he'll be back tomorrow. He'll bring twenty men if he has to. He can't afford to stay licked. There are too many people in Massacre who hate him and hate what he stands for."

One of the card players said nervously, "Watch your mouth, Snyder."

Hawks turned to glare at him. Then he nodded as if coming to his better senses. "Forget it," he mumbled, and went hurriedly back to the bar.

"You all right?" Sanderson asked Boone Ralston.

"I guess so." The words came raggedly.

"All right, let's get you home."

Young Ralston lurched around the table, his feet refusing to track quite properly. Sanderson took his arm and steered him the length of the room. No one said anything, no one stirred until they had reached the door and stepped out into the night.

Sanderson paused, still half sheltered by the doorway, looking sharply up and down the dark street. He would not have been surprised if Stover had planted a bushwacker. But nothing moved.

The town seemed to be buried in sleep. The noise from the saloon apparently had not disturbed the residents. There was no one in sight, not even the marshal.

Sanderson said, "What about a doctor?"

"I'm all right." The sharp fresh air seemed to have revived the boy. "I — thanks."

"Forget it."

"I can't forget it. You saved my life. Stover would have killed me if you hadn't been there. Somehow he found out."

"Found out what?"

"That I've thrown in with Ellen Jenner. That we were going to fight them."

"Fight who?"

"Colonel Peters. He runs the valley."

"Who is he?"

The boy shrugged. "He came up here from Texas, years ago. He and my grandfather drove the first herds into the valley."

"What happened to your grandfather?"

"Dead. A horse fell on him."

"And your father?"

"They murdered him."

"And your ranch?"

"It's covered with Peters's cattle," Boone Ralston said bitterly. "Now do you see why I offered you a job? We're collecting a crew, a fighting crew. You're just the man we need."

"I think not," Sanderson said. He started to add something, thought better of it, turned, and moved along the dark street toward the hotel.

Four

Like most small towns Massacre had no real need for a newspaper. Very little happened within the confines of the place that did not become general knowledge within a few hours.

Bert Oxford, the marshal, was waiting beside the high desk when Jim Sanderson came down the hotel stairs. The morning sun through the side windows lighted the dusty lobby, cruelly exposing the worn chairs and scarred floor.

The marshal noted that Sanderson carried his bedroll and his solid face relaxed in obvious relief. "Riding on?"

"Probably." Sanderson meant to ask some questions about Craig, but he had small hope that the man he sought had lingered in this valley.

"Breakfast?"

"I'll try Mary Ralston's. She was nice enough to serve me last night. I owe her that." He laid the room key on the desk.

"Hear you had a little trouble last night?"

Sanderson turned to Oxford deliberately. "I didn't see you around any place."

A dull flush darkened the man's wind-weathered cheeks. "No one sent for me."

Sanderson let it go. Why quarrel with Oxford? They would likely not see each other again. He walked the lobby's length, knowing that he had made an enemy and not caring, and came out into the freshness of the street.

The wind had died during the night, and the sun was hot enough to make him regret the sheep-lined coat.

He crossed the wide rutted street at an angle toward the restaurant. Inside, three men at the small counter gaped at him as he hung his coat on a peg and propped the bedroll below it. He took his seat. The girl came from the kitchen and looked surprised.

"Well!" she said. "Good morning!"

He returned the greeting and ordered. The three customers finished their coffee and departed, a bit reluctantly, their curiosity about Sanderson unsatisfied.

He sat, staring moodily at the wall until Mary Ralston returned with his bacon and eggs. "After what you ate last night I don't see how you can hold anything more," she said.

He grinned. "I have a mite of catching up to do."

She stood silent as he sugared the coffee and attacked his plate. "I'm glad you came in. It gives me a chance to thank you for what you did for my brother last night."

He did not answer. There seemed very little to say.

"Boone's young," she said. "He's hot headed and impatient, but he should know enough to keep out of Dred Stover's way."

"Why should he keep out of anyone's way?" he asked mildly. "Seems to me Boone had as much right in that saloon as Stover did."

She said, quickly, too quickly, "That's the trouble with men. All they think about is their rights. My father was the same, always talking about his rights, always saying they couldn't do that to him. So, he's dead."

Her black eyes were steady on him. There was no sign of grief. "I don't want that to happen to Boone."

He nodded. "Understandable."

"Is it?" She was studying his strong, lean face. "It's strange. I know almost nothing about you and what I do know isn't encouraging."

"What do you mean by that?"

She hesitated. "I shouldn't have said anything."

"Why not? You saved my life with food, remember." He smiled to encourage her. "Therefore it belongs to you, and you're privileged to say anything you like."

"Well, I meant that you came over the mountains, through all the snow. Only a man who was in a great hurry, who was probably running from something, would do such a thing."

"Go on."

"And then, well, you got into that fight at the saloon. Sure, I know. You probably saved Boone's life, at least he thinks you did. And you licked those men who've never been beaten before. That shows you're used to fighting, that you've had experience."

His smile grew a little wider. "You're making out a very bad case against me."

She flushed, but she went on steadily. "I have a reason for saying these things, Mr. Sanderson. In spite of what I've said I find that I trust you."

"Thank you, and the name is Jim."

She ignored this. "I trust you, and I am going to ask a favor. Boone has decided that you're the greatest person in the world. He kept me up half the night telling about you, and he might be impressed if you talked to him. He absolutely refuses to listen to me."

He finished his coffee and reached for tobacco. "What is it you want him told?"

"He's fixing to join Ellen Jenner in a fight against Colonel Peters and the Box P. Ellen's been recruiting gunmen for the last few weeks. Everyone in the valley knows it and Stover's crew have attacked her place twice. They got driven off both times, but that doesn't mean she has a chance to win."

"If you thought she did have a chance," Sanderson said, "would that change your thinking?"

Mary Ralston shook her dark head. "It wouldn't. Oh, I'm not trying to be noble about this. I hate Peters and Stover as thoroughly as Ellen Jenner does, and for better reason. But I saw my father murdered, and his crew killed or driven out, and our place burned down. I know what a range war is and what it will do to this valley. I can't bear to go through it again.

"Boone's too young to realize what it means. He was only ten when my father died. I was fifteen and we both would have starved if Mrs. Oxford hadn't taken us into the hotel and let me work for our room and food."

Sanderson had the picture of the girl, alone, almost helpless in this frontier town, carrying on, working to support her brother and herself. Mrs. Oxford, he judged from what little he had seen of her, would not be an easy person to work for, and he suspected that it had been less kindness and more a desire for cheap labor which had prompted the marshal's wife to take in the two children.

He said, "One thing I don't quite understand. Why does this Ellen Jenner, whoever she is, want Boone to join her? As you say, he's not much more than a boy, and if she has a crew of tough gunmen certainly Boone won't be enough more help to make it important."

"You'd have to understand conditions in this valley to see why it's important to her. First, the Jenners aren't much better liked than Colonel Peters. Her father came in here twenty years ago and bought out half a dozen homesteads at the north end of the valley.

"No one paid much attention to him. My father was busy fighting Peters and although there were rumors that Kane Jenner was not above buying a few head of rustled cattle, or running his iron on a maverick, they let him alone. The Jenner crew has always been a tough bunch, and the men who hide back in the hills have always made the Jenner ranch a kind of hangout."

"Sounds as if she and Peters are much alike."

"That's right, they are. But this spring Peters decided that if he held the whole valley it would be a lot simpler. He offered to buy Ellen out, and when she refused he had his men start moving her cattle north. The valley is mostly open range except for the water."

"You still haven't explained why she needs Boone."

"I'm coming to that. As I say, the valley people don't much like the Jenners and in a fight between Peters and Ellen they wouldn't take sides. We still have some friends here, people who feel that Boone and I got a bad deal. She thinks that if Boone is riding with her some of those people will line up on her side when the showdown comes. She's wrong, but it's the way she thinks. She even came in here and tried to get me to close this place and move out to her ranch. It's too bad she and her father didn't make that offer ten years ago when I needed help. But they didn't. I guess they figured that with my father out of the way they could move out and grab part of what had been our range."

"I see."

"There's more. Here along the creek there's plenty of water, but further north there's very little. Our spring is about the only good water in the whole central valley."

"You mean you still own it?"

"Yes, I've paid taxes every year. You see, my father homesteaded the spring and three hundred and twenty acres where our house was. The house is gone, burned, and the fences are torn down and Peters's cattle use the spring and the tanks my father built, but legally they still belong to Boone and me. So, if Boone rides with the Jenner crew it looks as if Ellen is helping him to recover something that is really ours."

"I guess she would be."

The girl shook her head. "Suppose they beat Peters, and drive his cattle off our old range. What happens then? We have no stock and no money to buy any. The land doesn't belong to us. It's open to anyone. So who profits? Ellen Jenner. Her cattle range out onto new grass and sooner or later she takes over in the valley in place of Peters. Does that make sense?"

It made very good sense.

"Where can I find Boone?" Sanderson asked. "I'll talk to him."

Impulsively she reached across the counter and laid her hand on his. "Thank you. Thank you very much. Would you — would you try to persuade him to go with you when you ride out? As long as he stays in this valley there will always be trouble. Sooner or later he'll be killed."

"I thought," he said gently, "that you had some doubts about me."

She looked directly into his eyes. "I have — had, that is. When I talk to you they seem to disappear. But even if you're running from the law I'd rather Boone went with you and had a chance to live. If he stays here on the Massacre death will surely catch him too soon."

He had the sudden temptation to tell her about Craig, and Will Austin, and the girl Sanderson had meant to marry. But before he could speak there was noise at the door and Boone Ralston came in and the chance was lost.

At sight of him the boy's face lighted and he came forward eagerly. "Sanderson, I was afraid you'd already gone."

"I seldom ride on an empty stomach if I can avoid it," Jim Sanderson said, "and your sister's cooking is the best advertisement for Massacre I've found."

"Sure, she can cook," Boone said, and hurried on. "The whole town is talking about you, or did you know?"

Sanderson had guessed as much. He was used to small towns.

"Doc Bertch says Stover's arm is broken in two places. I guess he won't be pulling a gun for a few days."

Sanderson sighed.

"Listen, I've got a friend I want you to meet, Sanderson. This is important." The boy sounded excited. "She's down at the livery, waiting."

Jim Sanderson met Mary Ralston's eyes and tried to convey a message: Trust me. I'll get him out of town, out of this valley if I can.

She understood. It seemed that they had developed a method of communication between them which did not require words.

"Come on, she's waiting," Boone said. "I told her I'd try and find you, but I didn't expect you to be here."

Sanderson rose. "All right."' He picked up his bedroll and followed the boy down the room to the door. He turned then, smiling at the girl, and she managed to smile in return.

Outside, Boone waited for him to catch up. "You remember I offered you a job last night? Well, my partner wants to talk to you."

"Your partner?"

"Ellen Jenner. You don't understand about this valley. You couldn't, of course, being so new here. But those men you whipped last night — they work for Colonel Peters. He murdered my father and ran my sister and me off our place, and now he's gone after Ellen. But he made a mistake. Ellen isn't like my sister. Ellen will fight. No one's going to run over her, and that includes Val Peters or Dred Stover."

"Look," Sanderson said, "this is none of my business, but I was talking to your sister."

He saw the boy freeze, saw the life go out of the young face leaving it almost mask- like. "You've got to understand Mary." He said this in a monotone, without feeling. "She's had it rough. When Dad was killed I was too young to help. She raised me and now she can't get it through her head that I'm grown up."

Sanderson did not say anything.

"She's seen trouble, plenty of trouble," the boy went on, "and it took the heart out of her. She can't think of anything except that I might be killed. She can't understand that I'd rather be dead than sitting here watching Peters's men ride over our place, watching his cows eat our grass."

Sanderson said, "I'm a little older than you are. I've seen trouble, and I don't like it. Supposing you did win back your home place, supposing you did drive Peters's stock away from your spring and off your grass. What would you do? You haven't any cows."

The boy was triumphant. "You think I haven't considered that? You're wrong. Ellen will stake us to a thousand head of she stock and calves. Three years from now there will be Lazy R stock all over the old range."

Sanderson looked at him, then away. How did you argue with a kid like Boone Ralston? Maybe he was right. Maybe Ellen Jenner would stake him. Mary Ralston could be wrong.

Walking toward the livery he wished silently that he had never met either Boone Ralston or his sister. He found himself attracted to them as he had been attracted to few people, but he also had something else to think about. His life was dedicated to bringing Craig to justice. There was no turning aside. He knew that he could never live at peace with himself until he settled the score with the murderer of Will Austin and Martha Horn.

He saw half a dozen mounted men around the entrance to the livery runway. From habit he appraised them and did not like what he saw.

Riders might be poorly dressed, might even have broken boots, but a man with pride cared for his saddle and his horse. These men were slovenly, their horses poorly groomed, their saddles makeshift affairs, some bound together by rawhide.

They shifted to permit his passage as he followed Boone into the barn, and a moment later Sanderson had his first look at Ellen Jenner.

Her appearance startled him. The girl's corn colored hair escaped from under a flat crowned man's hat. Her face was pink and white, round, with the largest blue eyes he had ever seen. The eyes were all the more striking because of their frame of dark curling lashes which did not seem to fit with either her hair or her complexion.

She came forward, her hand outstretched like a man's, a leather quirt swinging from the loop around her wrist, her eyes smiling, her mouth red and warm and inviting. "You must be Sanderson," she said. "I couldn't mistake you. Boone said you were the finest looking man he had ever seen."

Her voice was warm and husky, her hand solid in his grasp, and Sanderson knew that he would not have been human if her presence had not stirred him.

"Thank you," he said.

"And Boone tells me you're going to join us."

He opened his mouth to speak, and then he stopped, for a dark haired man came out of the office and spoke to the girl.

"There are four horses in back that will do," the man said.

Sanderson closed his mouth slowly. Here was Al Craig. Here was the man he had followed for five hundred miles.

Five

Craig was nearly as tall as Sanderson, but more lightly built, his wrists small, his hands almost like a woman's. He was dark, handsome in a bold way with hair that curled from under the side of his hat. A small horseshoe scar marred his left cheek and this scar made Sanderson certain of his identification. He had never seen the man, but he had seen good photographs, and there could be no mistake.

He heard the girl say, "This is Al Boston, Mr. Sanderson," and saw the man extend a slight hand. He hesitated an instant before he grasped it. This was the hand which had killed Martha Horn and sent Will Austin to his crashing death.

He wanted to jerk the man to him, to free his gun and beat it over the murderer's head. But he schooled himself to say casually, "How are you?" and return the small pressure of Craig's fingers and then drop his hand.

He had no fear that Craig would recognize him. He had been two hundred miles away from Toprock on the night when Craig had shot from ambush, his first bullet striking Martha Horn as she came from the hotel doorway, his second smashing its way through Will Austin's head.

The girl's death had been an accident; no doubt about that. Craig had been waiting for Austin, knowing that the stock detective had traced the bunch of stolen horses to him. He had shot at a moving shadow. But accident or not, she was dead, and this man had killed her.

Ellen Jenner said, "All right, Al. We'll take them. Get one of the other boys to help you." She turned to Sanderson. "I want to talk to you. Come into the office."

The livery office was a jumbled place. Feed was stacked in sacks at the far end, old saddles and pieces of harness were strung around as if the owner had started to repair them and then dropped them before he finished the job.

The girl walked across to the chair before the ancient rolltop and dropped into it, catching the weighted handle of the quirt in her gloved fingers and beating its braided lash lightly across her left palm.

"I heard about your fight with Stover. Shame you didn't break his neck instead of his arm." She said this pleasantly, without anger or feeling.

Sanderson thought fast. He could step into the runway and arrest Craig now, and take him to the marshal. He had a warrant for the man tucked away inside his shirt, but it was a Utah warrant. This was Colorado and it might be some time before he got cooperation from the state authorities.

He wondered what would happen if he tried it. The girl's crew was as tough looking a bunch of hardcases as he had seen in a long time and he was willing to bet that Boone Ralston was the only man among them not wanted somewhere for something.

How would they react when they learned that he was a detective in the employee of the Cattlemen's Association? They were his natural enemies. They probably hated all law officers, but undoubtedly most of them reserved a private hate for the men who rode the range in the pay of the Association.

Craig could not have been in this valley more than a week or ten days at most, but he was now a member of the Diamond J crew and as such could expect some help from his fellows. Not that any of this breed wasted much time in fighting the battles of others, but they did stick together against any law officer, reasoning that each one of them could easily find himself in a like spot and in need of help from the others.

No, he would have difficulty taking Craig now. Even the girl would oppose the action. Mary Ralston was very right about this Ellen Jenner. She demanded her own way and she would fight for what she desired. She needed this gun crew and she was wise enough to realize that they would stand by her only so long as she stood by them.

If she allowed one of their number to be taken, the rest would quietly slip away, to be seen no more in this valley.

But now that Sanderson had found Craig he had no intention of letting the man get away from him. This seemed to leave him no choice but to join forces with Ellen Jenner, to wait his chance, and take Craig when he got him away from the others.

Jim Sanderson had served the law too long simply to shoot Craig. Much as he hated the man and wanted to see him dead, his revenge would be legal. He would take Craig back and make him stand trial.

Sanderson was not a Mormon, but he had worked among the Saints long enough to have a high respect for their honesty and justice, and he knew that once Craig was returned to Toprock the legal machinery of the local court would handle the rest.

He heard the girl say, "I suppose Boone has told you what I'm up against? Why I'm hiring men?"

He nodded.

Her tone was still casual. "I understand you're interested in staying a jump or so ahead of something."

"I haven't said so."

She laughed and the sound filled the cluttered room. "Boone says you came over the ridge. You didn't ride through all that snow for exercise."

"I could have been following somebody."

She considered this, studying him. "I think not. You're a smart one, Sanderson. It shows. You'd have had to want a man pretty bad to risk the mountains at this time of year."

"All right." He tried to make his tone sullen. "So I'm running. So I'll keep on running."

"I don't care what you're running from. Would it surprise you if I said that my father was wanted in half a dozen states before he settled here? All my life we've run a grubline for every outlaw who drifted in

70

out of the brush. I was raised with owl-hoots. Does that make you feel better?"

"Maybe."

They studied each other like two gamblers about to start a poker hand, and after a long moment she said, "I need someone like you almost as much as you need a place to hide. There are only five men in my regular crew, and they're a poor lot. I've hired twelve extra hands, and the less said about them the better. You saw some of them as you came in."

He waited, poker-faced.

"I need a man who can control them. They're like a bunch of coyotes, each thinking mainly of himself. I want someone who can whip them into a fighting crew."

"What makes you think I'm the man?"

Her smile turned a little mocking. "Save the modesty for those it might impress. I think you are and I know that you think you are. They've all heard what you did to Dred Stover and that really impresses them. Most of them, the ones who have been hanging around this country for any spell, know Stover and hate him and fear him."

"So what's in it for me?"

"Protection."

He laughed. "You'll have to do better than that, Miss Jenner. You already said I handled Stover. That should prove I can take care of myself."

"A hundred a month and found." It was twice as much as a foreman got, three times what an ordinary rider could hope to draw. She needed him, all right, and he didn't want to hesitate too long; that would give her the idea he had trouble making up his mind.

"I'll take it," he said. "Now, what am I supposed to do to earn it?"

"Drive Peters out of the valley," she said steadily. "Kill him if you have to. Make the valley mine."

He smiled gently at her.

"I thought you were fighting to hold your place — and Boone's," he said.

Her eyes veiled then, but he had caught the flash. Ellen Jenner was not fighting for the Ralstons' right to return to their ranch. She was fighting for nobody but Ellen Jenner.

"I spoke too quickly," she said. "I meant only that as long as Peters is in the valley no one else is safe. The old fool is mad. Nothing is important to him except having his own way. You'll find out soon enough."

The knock came almost as an answer to

her words. The door swung open and a grey haired man thrust his head in.

"The Colonel and half a dozen riders just came in," he said.

At once Ellen Jenner came to her feet, her mouth tightening until her soft lips looked bruised with pressure.

"All right, Sanderson. You get action quicker than I thought. This is your chance to see the man you're fighting — and to see if the crew will stand with you."

She moved swiftly into the runway and along it to the big double front door. Her men, who had been loitering in a fan-shaped group when Sanderson came in, had drawn together like steers at sight of a wolf. They split to let the girl and Sanderson pass, then shifted back uneasily, filling the doorway behind them.

Ellen Jenner stopped at the edge of the sidewalk, staring northward up the street. A block away a buckboard drawn by matched horses came slowly toward them, followed by half a dozen mounted men.

Sanderson looked around. The way his crew was bunched, the barn doorway was almost an invitation for attack. He gave his first order as the foreman of the Diamond J.

"Boone, get a rifle, get up in the hay

mow and cover the street. You —" he pointed to a yellow haired man at the rear — "go around the corner of the building and cover us from there. Two of you stay in this doorway. The rest of you drift back to the alley and ease up on both sides of them when they stop."

They grinned at him, the uncertainty and unease fading from their faces. Then they separated and slipped quickly out of sight. The girl had not turned. She stood quiet, her only movement being the light tapping of her quirt against the open palm of her left hand.

Sanderson felt a small thrill of admiration. The girl acted as if she owned the town and the valley; as if the Colonel and his men rode toward her only by sufferance.

He shifted three long steps to the right. She gave him a mocking smile.

"You don't have to get me out of the line of fire," she said.

He did not answer. He watched the progress of the buckboard, the horses stepping daintily as if they found the rutted street far from their liking, the riders fanning out a little until they covered the width of the street.

One man alone rode in the buckboard and as he drew closer Sanderson realized that he was very old. He was dressed in black, his hat wide-brimmed, its crown soft and flat. His coat was a frock affair reaching almost to his knees, and he wore a white shirt and flowing tie, not common in the country.

"Quite a dude." Sanderson said it softly, but the words carried to Ellen Jenner and she gave him another amused smile.

"From all accounts he was, sixty years ago."

The Colonel had spotted them standing before the stable and swung his team over to the wrong side of the street, so that when he halted the buckboard before them, he was only half a dozen feet away.

He sat there, his grey hair showing a struggling edge beneath the shelter of his hat brim, his beak of a nose and age-dried face making him look something like a bird wearing a black hat.

"You." He pointed at Sanderson with a bony finger. "You broke Dred's arm last night."

Sanderson did not answer. The Colonel turned his head. As he did so Sanderson realized how thin his neck was and how long, like a turkey gobbler's.

"Bob."

His riders had maintained their semicircle, swinging so that its points reached the sidewalk's edge on each side of the wagon and some thirty feet away. One of them rode up to the buckboard.

"Get the marshal," Peters said.

The man pivoted his horse and rode down toward the hotel. Ellen Jenner's laugh rang out over the dusty street.

"Colonel," she said, "this is the end and you aren't smart enough to know it. For years you've made the valley and the people in it crawl on their hands and knees for the crumbs you cared to throw. That day is over."

He sat there with his clothes hanging on his bony frame like a scarecrow from the fields. "I should have hung your daddy for the thief he was," he said.

"You should have," she told him, "but you didn't. You didn't think Kane Jenner was important enough to bother with. You broke the Ralstons and the others, but you let the Jenners alone to nurse their scrub cattle in the brush. Well, I'm here and you're going out."

"Am I?" He snorted. "I'd have cracked down on you last fall if you hadn't been a woman."

Her laughter filled the warm sunlit street. "That didn't stop you from running

Mary Ralston and her brother off their place and burning their house. You didn't jump the Diamond J because deep in your dried up heart you're afraid of me. You know I'm tougher than you are."

For a minute Sanderson thought the man in the buckboard would have a stroke. His thin face went purple and his gobbler neck seemed to swell. But somehow he got control of himself.

"You talk big," he said. "Your daddy talked big too. The Jenners were always long on air and short on performance. You've got some surprises coming, girl, you and your ragtail crew. I'll see every one of them hung or run into the brush, and I'll see you scrubbing floors if you can find anyone to hire you." He stopped. "Here comes the marshal."

Bert Oxford was indeed coming. He moved up the sidewalk slowly, a man embarked on an unpleasant errand, the rider who had been sent after him keeping pace on his horse as if he half expected that left to himself Oxford would turn and run.

Sanderson frowned a little. He had not counted on this move by the Colonel and he feared what it might lead to. He had no desire to kill the marshal, and he had no illusion that Oxford was a coward.

The man might walk the other way when he heard gunfire in a saloon as he had done on the preceding evening, but faced with a direct challenge of any kind he would not back down.

He came unhurriedly, his body swinging easily as if he were out for a leisurely stroll, and stopped beside the buckboard.

"You sent for me, Colonel?"

Peters swore at him. "Why didn't you arrest this man for attacking Stover, for breaking his arm?"

The marshal looked mildly surprised. "Did he do that?"

Ellen Jenner laughed again. Peters shifted on the seat. He reached out as if to catch up the whip, to strike the man on the sidewalk with its long lash, but he checked himself. "I'm telling you now," he said.

"You want to swear out a warrant?"

Again Peters seemed short of breath. When he finally managed speech it came out in a near shriek. "Who do you think got you this job, Bert? Who's kept your lazy hide in office all these years? Arrest that man now. Sure, I'll swear out a warrant. I'll swear out a dozen warrants."

"The judge is down at the courthouse. Get the warrant and I'll serve it."

"And let him get away while I'm gone? That's all I wanted to know, which side you're on, Bert. I know now."

The marshal's jaw took on a set look.

"I'm not on either side, Colonel."

"A man's for me or against me." Peters's voice was as decided as a closing steel trap. "All right, Bert, turn and walk away."

"No," the marshal said.

Watching him, Sanderson could almost read Bert Oxford's mind. Oxford would not have come down here if he had not been called. He preferred to let things settle themselves when he could. But now that he was here, some stubborn pride, some remnant of the man he once had been would not let him turn his back.

"All right, then." The man in the buggy had worked himself to the verge of frenzy. "Take them, boys! Take all of them, and if the female gets hit it's her own fault!"

Sanderson took half a step forward.

"Wait, old man."

The scrawny, black-garbed figure on the buckboard jerked as if stung by a wasp. Obviously no one had ever dared mention age to the Colonel before. The old man glared at Sanderson.

"What do you want?"

"Take a look at the hay door above your

head," Sanderson said. "Take a look at the building corners before you start something you can't finish."

The Colonel glanced upward. Then he twisted his head right and left, like an alert turkey gobbler. He saw the armed riders who had drifted casually around the corners of the weathered building, out-flanking his mounted men, while up above, Boone Ralston stood in the hay mow doorway, his rifle held ready.

Colonel Val Peters was no fool. He had spent a lifetime fighting, brawling with his neighbors, but he had never taken on a fight unless he thought the odds were in his favor. He sat solid on his seat, staring thoughtfully at the rumps of his matched team. Then he raised his voice.

"All right, boys, there'll be another day."

He started the team, swinging the horses in a wide circle, and headed out of town with his crew behind him.

From the corner of his eye Jim Sanderson caught movement. He grabbed Ellen Jenner's wrist just as she brought the light gun clear of its holster.

She struggled angrily but he gave her no chance. He twisted her arm until she cried out and let the gun slip from her fingers to the dust. He stooped, picked it up, emptied the cylinder and returned it to her, butt first.

"I should kill you for that," she said.

"If you'd fired that shot you'd have turned this whole street into a death trap."

"You fool! For once in my life I had Val Peters exactly where I wanted him. He was a duck, sitting up there to be shot. We'll never have that chance again."

She was beautiful, soft-looking, very much a woman in appearance. But Jim Sanderson realized that there was nothing soft in her. She was as predatory as a wolf.

"Maybe I'm not the man you're looking for," he said.

Anger still boiled in her, but she curbed it as she might have curbed a dangerous horse. When she spoke again she had herself under full control.

"Sanderson, you're a marked man now. Val Peters will never forget that you made him look silly before the town. No one ever has done that and lived. The few who ever tried were found with bullets in their backs out on a lonely trail."

"I'll keep that in mind," he said.

"You simply don't understand what we're up against. Fair play is something the Colonel never even heard of. Neither did Dred Stover or the men who ride under him. Killing a man is a job to be done, and they prefer doing it in a way that brings no danger to themselves."

"I see," he said.

"You'd better see," she said. "If you fight men like the Colonel you can't afford to be soft, even for an instant. You have to strike when the opportunity comes. Now let's ride."

Never in his life had Jim Sanderson ridden out on any errand with less enthusiasm. Even the sight of Al Craig, who now called himself Al Boston, brought no lift to his flagging spirits.

He had seen range wars. He knew what they were — grim, ruthless conflicts in which one side was probably as much to blame as the other, men shooting men because they happened to be riding for different outfits and for no other reason.

Seldom did justice or mercy intervene.

He mounted and looked at the motley crew gathered around him. Al Craig sat between the girl and the grizzled rider who was her foreman. Boone Ralston led a horse around the barn, swung up into the saddle and walked his mount to Sanderson's side.

His dark face, boldly chiseled and Indian-like in the bright sunlight, held a satisfied smile. "I never saw anything as funny as the Colonel's face when he looked up at the mow doorway and saw me squatting there with a rifle trained on his head. He looked as if he'd swallowed his Adam's apple."

Sanderson said soberly, "This isn't a joke, Boone."

Resentment flared in the young face. "Sure it's no joke. Ellen was right. We should have gotten the Colonel when the chance was there. Peters is no fool. He'll hole up at the ranch and we'll have to dig him out."

Sanderson started to say, "You couldn't just shoot him in the back," but stopped. The boy's father had been shot in the back. When hate takes over a country, any attack on the enemy seems to be right. He had seen the same thing happen on other ranges, many times before.

The marshal had not moved from his position on the sidewalk. Now he stepped down into the street dust and crossed to Sanderson.

"I judge you've thrown in with Ellen Jenner," he said quietly.

"Looks that way."

"I hope you don't live to regret it, but I think you will."

They watched each other without liking.

"But I want to warn you of one thing," Bert Oxford said, "just as I intend to warn the Colonel. Keep your fight out of this town. If you want to kill each other that's not my business and I suspect the valley would be better off if you were all dead. But I won't have the fight brought into town."

He walked back to the sidewalk and on down the street. Boone Ralston laughed harshly. "Old fool. What does he think he'd do about it?"

Sanderson did not answer. Ellen Jenner had already wheeled her horse and was riding down the street, her men falling in behind her. Boone and Sanderson wheeled into the end of the column and it paraded slowly for the three business blocks as if the girl in the lead was purposely making a show of strength to impress the towns-people they passed.

Before the restaurant Boone checked his pace. "Hold my horse a minute." He flipped the rein to Sanderson and swung down. Sanderson sat quiet, waiting. Through the building's front window he could see Boone arguing with his sister. Then the boy turned back to the door and Mary Ralston followed him onto the side-walk.

Her face had a drawn, bleak look, all the beauty gone, her eyes very dark, her mouth grim.

Jim Sanderson had a sudden desire to reassure her. He said, "Don't worry, I'll keep him out of trouble," but he could see that she did not believe him.

"I might have known that you couldn't resist Ellen Jenner," she said. "I don't blame you. Few men can. I guess all men were made to be fools." She turned, straight-backed, and went into the restaurant.

Six

The home ranch of the Diamond J was in a shallow canyon at the extreme northern end of the valley. The trail from Massacre led past the canyon's entrance, swinging eastward to skirt the foothills until it reached Snow canyon ten miles from the Diamond J. There it cut through the mountains to Fairview.

On the ride out to the ranch Sanderson had had Boone Ralston brief him on distances and on each side trail they passed. A man in a strange country was always at a heavy disadvantage.

Fifteen miles below the Diamond J, the road led past two wooden posts which stood gauntly with faint wagon tracks running between them, then climbed a small hillock and vanished toward the valley bench.

"Where's that lead?" Sanderson pointed to the faint trace.

Boone checked his horse. He sat the saddle quietly, not speaking for a full minute; then as if on impulse he swung his horse between the weathered posts. "Come on, I'll show you."

They had been lagging behind the column of riders and no one ahead paid any attention as they rode off the trail, following it to the top of the hill a good half-mile from the road's edge. At the top Boone Ralston checked his pace and pointed to the small meadow beyond.

Timber ran down here from the higher bench and made a backdrop for the stone chimney which stood alone in the charred shambles scattered around its base.

Beyond the chimney a huge spring broke out of the bench, its crystal water flashing in the sun, running down in a network of earth ditches to three tanks below the ruin of the house.

Sanderson did not need to see the pain on Boone's face to realize where they were.

"Your place," he said.

Boone nodded. Half a dozen steers were grazing beyond the tanks and without a word the boy pulled his horse around and rode toward them. Sanderson did not guess his intent until Boone reached down, pulled the rifle from beneath his leg and swung it up. Before Sanderson could stop him he had killed one steer after another until they lay scattered, their tan and white markings making a color pattern against the greenness of the spring grass.

It was a senseless, purposeless thing to do, the act of an angry child, striking out against those who had hurt him.

He shoved the rifle back into its boot savagely, saying as he did so, "There are six Box P critters that won't eat any more Ralston grass. I'll shoot any Peters stock I see." He swung the horse around and spurred back toward the road, not waiting for Sanderson to follow.

Before Boone reached the roadway, Ellen Jenner and the rest of the crew came pounding toward them. The girl hauled up in a cloud of dust.

"Who fired those shots?"

"I did." He checked his horse and sat the saddle in sullen silence until Sanderson rode up. The girl looked from one to the other. "What were you shooting at?"

"Some Peters cattle. I saw them eating our grass."

She said calmly, "That wasn't very smart. Peters is going to have another charge to make against us."

Boone stared at her. "But Ellen, what do you care about charges? You were ready to shoot Peters in town."

She gave Sanderson a long, studying look, and then without speaking further swung her horse and headed down the road, the crew stretching out behind her.

Boone glanced at Sanderson, noting his neutral expression. "You think I'm a fool, don't you?"

The older man shrugged. "It was something that had no purpose in it."

Boone shook his head. "It did something to me, seeing those Box P steers, eating where my cattle ought to be. I guess I went a little crazy." He swung away, riding after the crew, and Sanderson followed more slowly, in an increasingly troubled mood.

The more he saw of this setup, the less he liked it. But he couldn't get out of the mess, without taking Al Craig with him, and until the big chance came he would just have to string along.

The ranch buildings of the Diamond J made a blotch of grey against the greenness of the canyon floor and of the timber which grew thickly down the canyon walls.

The squared logs had weathered to a kind of silver in the rain and sun and wind, and the mud which chinked their cracks heightened the effect.

Kane Jenner had chosen his site well. The land on both sides of the small canyon was too rough for a horse to cross easily. Anyone wanting to attack the place would be forced either to come in through the narrow opening of the canyon mouth or climb on foot the rocky hillside, so steep in most places that a man had to crawl to keep his balance.

A trail led from the rear of the buildings, footing its twisting way upward toward the tumbled peaks above, too narrow for two people to ride abreast.

Boone Ralston pointed out the trail as they unsaddled their horses and turned them into the corral. "That leads back to Crawford's," he said.

"What's Crawford's?"

"Store, saloon. It's a kind of head-quarters for the brush riders. Most of the men here came from Crawford's. It's a tough place."

Sanderson carried his saddle across to place it on the fence and turned to look at the ranch layout. The main house looked more like a fort than a dwelling place. The solid log walls must be a good eighteen inches thick and the windows were like slits in a blockhouse.

It sat back so that the rear wall almost

touched a rocky face which rose up at a sharp angle to a height of several hundred feet.

Below it, toward the canyon's mouth, the bunkhouse, the cookshack and dining room and the sheds were arranged in a semi-circle like the outer works of an ancient castle, serving as cover in case attackers attempted to enter the canyon mouth.

Ellen Jenner was standing to one side, talking to the grey-haired man who was her regular foreman. She motioned and Sanderson moved toward them, trailed by Boone who did not seem to want to be left by himself.

"This is Ford Patton," she told Sanderson. "He's been foreman for fifteen years."

Sanderson shook hands. The man's face was long and narrow, and his eyes, set very close to the high bridge of his nose, never seemed to look directly at the person to whom he was speaking.

"How are yuh?" he mumbled, and the resentment in the voice told Sanderson that Patton did not relish the idea of someone pre-empting the place he had held so long.

"Ford is still foreman of the old crew."

Ellen Jenner said this very distinctly. "He and the regular riders will look after the cattle."

Had Sanderson taken the coming fight with personal seriousness he would have objected to the arrangement. You could not divide a crew into two parts and not have constant friction. But since his real purpose in being at the ranch was merely to get Al Craig away from the crew, he said nothing.

"Ford will show you where to bunk." Ellen turned as if dismissing them all from her mind and walked to the steps of the ranch house's long gallery.

Sanderson watched her for a moment, and then found Ford Patton watching him. He caught a glint of malice in the narrow eyes.

"Think you'll like it here?" Patton said.

Sanderson's shrug was noncommittal. "I've been in worse places. Where do we sleep?"

Patton led them to the bunkhouse. It was a single room, the bunks in tiers of two along both walls, a pot bellied stove at the far end and a small room beyond the stove which was obviously for the foreman's use.

"Kind of crowded. We don't usually have a big crew."

Undoubtedly the ranch had never before employed as large a crew, but when Kane Jenner had first built the place he had included space for chance riders in considerable numbers.

About half the men were in the room, five of them already playing cards at a table beside the stove, the others sitting on their bunks, talking in low voices. The talking ceased as the two bosses came in and Sanderson knew that every man in the place was sizing him up, forming his own opinion of the new ramrod.

Patton walked half the length of the room and indicated two upper bunks whose ticks showed no blankets. "Take your choice."

Al Craig was sitting in the lower bunk beneath one of the empties. He looked up as they stopped before him, his eyes like bright licorice buttons.

Sanderson considered him. "Your name's Boston?"

Craig's head moved slightly.

"You take the upper bunk."

Quick resentment lifted the man to his feet. He stood facing Sanderson, his body bent a little forward, his right hand hovering over his holstered gun.

"Who says so?"

"I do."

"To hell with you. I was here first."

Sanderson's right hand snaked out to catch the front of the man's shirt. He jerked him forward until only inches separated them. His left hand shot downward and grasped Craig's wrist as the man tried to draw his gun.

They stood thus, testing strength as Craig tried to raise the gun in spite of Sanderson's restraining hand.

Everyone in the bunkhouse watched in silence, and Sanderson could feel the hostility in the room behind him. He did not care. His only purpose was to make life at the ranch so unbearable for Craig that the man would ride on. Once away from the ranch he could take him prisoner.

"Damn you." Craig relaxed suddenly as if realizing the hopelessness of the uneven struggle.

Sanderson released the wrist and stepped back.

"Move those blankets to the upper bunk," he said.

Instead of obeying, Al Craig went for his gun. Sanderson had expected him to do just that. His own weapon was suddenly in his hand and some of the hate he felt for the man got into his voice.

"Go ahead, lift it free."

Craig looked as if he would rather pull that gun than do anything else in the world. But somewhere between the brain and the muscles which controlled his arm a valve shut and he stood, frozen, unable to lift it farther.

"Pull it or move those blankets," Sanderson said.

Craig let the gun drop back into the leather. He turned stiffly, his motions as uncoordinated as a drunk's, and began to strip the bedding from the lower bunk.

Behind them there was no sound. The card players at the table by the stove sat motionless, cardboards forgotten in their hands, watching the new foreman.

Sanderson dropped his gun back into the holster.

"Anyone have anything to say?" he inquired mildly.

They just sat there.

"All right," he said. "Just remember one thing, all of you. I give the orders here, and when I give one I expect a man to jump. The one who doesn't gets hurt."

He waited. Still they didn't move. Then as if satisfied he glanced at Boone Ralston.

"When Craig gets that bunk stripped," he said, "fix my blankets."

He saw Ralston's blink of surprise. It

was no real part of his plan to ride the boy, but he wanted the crew to understand that Ralston was no particular pet of his. The boy would be safer that way, because if the crew got sore enough at the foreman they might take out their anger on someone they suspected was his "pet".

He walked out of the bunkhouse into the yard. Ford Patton followed him. He halted in the hard baked yard and Patton stopped at his side.

"That wasn't necessary," the old foreman said.

"I think it was."

"Then you're a fool," Patton said.

"Old man," Sanderson said, "you run your affairs and I'll run mine. Those men in there are little better than dogs. There are two ways to handle dogs. Good ones you can tame by kindness, bad ones you have to use a whip on. Those men are bad. They wouldn't understand kindness. They'd think you were weak."

Patton said savagely, "You've got it all figured out, haven't you?"

"I figured that out a long time before I ever saw this valley or this fight."

"That's the trouble," the foreman said. "This fight to you is just another fight. When it's finished, no matter how it ends, you'll climb on your horse and ride out, looking for another valley, looking for another rancher who will hire your gun."

"And you?"

"I've been on this ranch for years. I helped raise that girl up at the house. I'm interested in what becomes of her."

Sanderson rubbed his chin thoughtfully. "From what I hear, Jenner's operation has never been too clean."

A dull flash darkened Patton's wind-blown cheeks. "Let me tell you something. Kane Jenner had his faults. We may have run our brand on some calves that maybe weren't ours, but we never went in for wholesale rustling. When a man gets older he learns things that you don't think of when you're young. Ellen started this fight. I admit it. I know she's wrong, but how do you live with a grizzly bear? That's what Val Peters is. He reaches out for everything in sight. You have to stand against him or be wiped out and he's finally gotten around to us."

Sanderson just grunted.

"So we rise or fall on the gunmen she's hired," Patton said. "You're right, they're dogs, but we need them, and you can't expect a man to fight for you when you kick him in the stomach."

"I'll handle them my way," Sanderson said calmly.

For a moment he thought Patton would draw on him. The desire flared in the old man's eyes. Then he swung on his heel and headed for the main house.

Sanderson watched him, a slow smile tugging at his lips. Boone Ralston came from the bunkhouse and walked to his side. The boy's face was troubled and Sanderson felt a little sorry for him.

"Look, Jim." It was the first time Boone had used his first name. "That's a bad crowd in there and they didn't like the way you handled Al Boston."

Sanderson shrugged.

"Don't misunderstand me," Boone said, and he sounded very earnest, almost desperate. "After what you did in the saloon last night I'd follow you from hell to breakfast. I figure you had a reason for what you did, but we need those men."

That, thought Sanderson, was the keynote to the whole situation. He had been so absorbed in his own problem that he had lost sight of the situation in the valley. Boone Ralston hoped to recover what was legally and morally his. The fact that Sanderson did not believe Ellen Jenner would ever allow the Ralstons to return to their ranch even if Val Peters was driven out did not mean that Boone had no rights.

He started to say something, but Ellen Jenner came out onto the ranch porch, trailed by Patton, and sent her call across the yard.

"Sanderson, I want to talk to you."

He went toward her. As he reached the steps leading up to the porch he saw the pleased anticipation on the old foreman's face. But if Patton had planned to be present at the interview, the girl had decided otherwise. She dismissed him with a nod.

"I'll talk to you later, Ford. Sanderson, come into the house."

He walked past Patton and into the wide hallway. The hall ran straight back to a kitchen which he could see through the open doorway. To the right was a room that apparently served as both a living room and a ranch office.

He glanced around, at the desk in the far corner, at the gear scattered on the chairs and a wide table, more a man's room than a woman's, and he suspected that it had not changed much since the girl's father died.

Ellen Jenner said, "What are you trying to do, Sanderson?"

"Whip the crew into shape."

"Was it necessary to pick a fight with Al Boston?"

"Boston's a troublemaker. The sooner he rides on, the better."

"Boston's a man," she said quietly. "And he knows how to use a gun. Isn't that about all we can expect of any of them?"

He shrugged. "I either run the crew my way, or I don't run it. The choice is yours. It's as simple as that."

"I'm not so sure."

"What do you mean?"

She considered a long time before answering. "There isn't a great deal I miss, Jim Sanderson. I saw you start this morning when Boston came out of the livery office, as if you were surprised to see him. Tell me, what's between you and Boston?"

She caught Sanderson off guard, but he covered quickly.

"I never saw the man before in my life."

Her expression said that she did not believe him. "Boone told me you came over the ridge. So did he."

They watched each other like two fencers. Then her tone changed. "I'm not trying to pry into your business. I don't care anything about Boston, or any of the

100

rest of the crew. All I care about is beating the Colonel and driving him out of the valley."

Sanderson did not answer and she came a step toward him and reached out to put her hands on his shoulders. "Look at me."

He did.

"I'm not bad looking, am I?"

He smiled a little. "You're beautiful."

"No," she said, "I'm not beautiful, but I'm attractive. I know it. Enough men have told me so. Enough men have wanted to marry me."

There seemed to be nothing to say.

"Do you know why I haven't married? I'll tell you why. I won't marry until I find a man as strong or stronger than I am. I mean to own this valley, to run it as it should be run. There isn't any better feed in the whole West than on the Massacre. The Diamond J can be one of the great ranches of the world, but it needs strong hands to guide it, a determined man who isn't afraid to take what he wants. When I first saw you, I thought you might be that man. Am I wrong?"

Sanderson had known a number of women during his life, but none quite like this girl. She was throwing herself at him, offering herself and her ranch if he was strong enough to take them and determined enough to hold them.

Her hands tightened on his shoulders. She was half a head shorter than he, but she lifted her face, all the animal vitality of her nature open in her eyes, in her upturned mouth.

He kissed her hard on the parted lips, closing his arms around her, feeling the warm strength of her body close against his. Yet, strangely, through it all he knew a certain detachment, as if he were sitting off to one side, watching this happen. Certainly he could still think well enough.

Why not take her? Why not take the valley, the ranch, the girl? Martha Horn was dead and nothing he could do would ever bring her back to him.

His life stretched ahead, an empty life, always riding on from one range to the next, running down one rustler after another, sitting in dusty, hot courtrooms, giving his evidence which would send prisoner after prisoner to the penitentiary.

Why not? The surge of sudden desire swept over him, bred as much of loneliness as of the pressure from her body.

She sensed the change in him, and a shudder seemed to run through her strong limbs. Then she pushed him away, laughing a little as if to remove the bait before the trap closed entirely.

"Not yet, Sanderson, not yet."

He knew a sudden rising anger, an anger at himself for having let himself be swayed, even for the instant. He had read her thoroughly at the first meeting and he had not been mistaken.

She was ruthless, selfish; there was nothing she would not do to accomplish what she chose.

"My mistake," he said soberly.

"No," she said. "Not a mistake." She stepped forward again, grasping his shoulders. "But you have to earn the right, first, Sanderson. Take the valley. Give it to me, then ask what you wish."

She tilted her face. He kissed her again, but this time he did it mechanically.

Seven

Darkness laid a veil across the canyon as Jim Sanderson came from the cook shack. The meal had been eaten in heavy silence, the crew showing their hostility by not raising their heads, not once speaking while he was in the room.

He walked down past the corral and stood staring thoughtfully at the canyon's mouth, then turned and looked at the rock face which rose behind the ranch house.

On impulse he moved back across the yard to the edge of the face, and thus discovered something which he had not seen before. Someone had cut steps up the face to the shelf above.

He climbed them slowly. At places the builder, whoever he had been, had taken advantage of the natural faults and crevices. At others the rock had been drilled out with the use of a singlejack.

When he reached the shelf he crossed it and examined the canyon wall beyond. It was steep, tree-studded, a jumble of broken rock and granite faces through which he doubted a man might make his way.

Then he turned and looked at the canyon below. This was a natural lookout post and he suspected that Kane Jenner and his men had used it as such many times.

He sat down on the lip, watching the yard, faintly visible in the semi-darkness. He saw a figure come from the bunkhouse, glance around, then move toward the main house.

Something furtive in the man's actions sharpened his attention, but he did not realize that it was Al Craig until the man crossed a band of light thrown from the ranch house window.

He stiffened, rising quickly to his feet as he saw Craig reach the steps and disappear from view. There could be no doubt that Craig had gone to talk to the girl, and Sanderson's mouth tightened. If she told Craig that she thought Sanderson had followed him into the valley the man would undoubtedly sneak away.

Sanderson felt that he had to know what was said between them. Quickly he made his way back down the rocky steps and circled the corner of the house to reach the end of the porch. He glanced around, saw no one in the yard, grasped the railing and lifted himself over it to the porch.

He stayed quiet for a moment, then moved along the log wall toward the lighted window of the front room. The window had been opened at the top a few inches to let in the warm afternoon air and had not been closed.

He had arrived in time to witness the encounter, but he was not prepared for what he saw and heard.

Ellen Jenner came forward and put both hands on Craig's shoulders. And then, almost word for word, she repeated what she had said to Sanderson in the afternoon.

"I'm going to take this valley," she said, "and I need a strong man to help me hold it. From the first time I saw you I thought you might be that man."

Sanderson had a side view of Craig's face. He saw the man smirk and slip his arms around the girl and bend to kiss her.

Sanderson retreated to the porch rail, stepped over it quietly and dropped to the ground, cutting away from the house until he reached the canyon side and then along it to the bunkhouse. Inside, two card games were going, amid much talk and laughter. It died as he stepped through the door.

Boone Ralston was stretched on his bunk, his hands under his dark head, his eyes closed. Sanderson walked to him and said so that the whole room could hear:

"Get your rifle and get up on that stone shelf behind the house. The moon will be up in half an hour and it should be clear enough to show you anyone who tries to come into the canyon."

Boone rolled over and sat up. "You think Peters will try and attack tonight? He's been beaten off twice."

"What would you do?"

The boy nodded. He swung down from his upper bunk and got his rifle.

"I'll send Boston to relieve you at midnight," Sanderson said. He wasn't afraid that the girl had told Craig about being followed over the ridge. She had been too busy binding the rider to her cause to say anything which might scare Craig into running further. "Where is Boston?" he added, addressing the crew in general.

Patton spoke from one of the card tables. "He went out fifteen minutes ago."

Sanderson grunted. He stripped off his coat, stretched on the bunk, closed his eyes. Every muscle in his big body ached.

The card games went on. Gradually, as if the crew forgot his presence, the noise increased. He dozed, and then the closing of the bunkhouse door roused him. Al Boston came along the row of bunks and paused, about to swing himself into the one above Sanderson.

Sanderson sat up. The man was smiling. The pleased look on his dark narrow face suggested that the world had just been handed to him on a silver salver.

Sanderson knew the source of Craig's pleasure. He believed everything Ellen Jenner had told him; he visualized himself as the new owner of the whole valley. Sanderson cursed the way things had broken. Now nothing would persuade Craig to leave the ranch.

Craig noticed that he was awake. He said, "I hope you like the bunk, ramrod."

Sanderson shrugged. "I've sent young Ralston up to that rock shelf behind the ranch house to keep watch. I want you to relieve him at midnight." The noise from the card tables had slackened and he knew that the players expected argument.

"Sure," Craig said matter-of-factly.

The rest of the crew did not understand the change. Sanderson did. He said, "You know how to get up there?"

Craig shook his head.

"Come on, I'll show you." They moved

together into the moonlit yard. The lights in the ranch house were out and they circled the building, walking to the steps which climbed across the rock face.

"Boone." Sanderson raised his voice. "Boone Ralston."

The answer came, not from the rock above but from the rear porch of the main house. "Here."

Sanderson spun around. He saw Boone step out of the shadows into the moonlight. But the boy was not alone. Ellen Jenner followed him.

He glanced quickly toward Al Craig, wondering if the outlaw had had the same thought which had flashed through his mind — that the girl, not content with her conquest of Sanderson and Craig, was now practicing her wiles on Ralston.

But Craig's face, showing plainly in the silvery glow, was serene. Apparently it did not dawn on him that he had any competition. He was too self-centered to believe that Ellen Jenner would consider another man after making an offer to him.

Boone sounded a little embarrassed. "Ellen saw me up on the ledge and wanted to know what I was doing."

Sanderson offered no comment. He said, "Craig will relieve you at midnight. If you see anything — anything at all that looks suspicious — one shot will bring us all."

He nodded to the girl and turned on his heel. Craig hesitated for a moment, then followed.

Sanderson did not know how long he had been asleep when the shot came, bringing the dark bunkhouse around him into excited life. He rolled from the bunk, fumbling for his boots. Someone had struck a match at the far end of the room and was cursing as he reached for a lamp. It sounded like Patton, but Sanderson could not be sure.

"Kill that light." The words cracked and the man dropped the match to the floor. Once in his boots Sanderson pulled the rifle from beneath his bunk and headed for the door. As he did so, four quick shots from the ledge brought answering fire from the mouth of the canyon.

He ran into three or four men in the darkness, all struggling into their clothes, and was glad that he had slept in everything but his boots.

Outside the moon was very bright, showing the buildings and the corral fence in sharp relief. He glanced toward the shelf, saw Boone Ralston outlined against the darker rock, and swore softly as half a dozen shots spewed from the canyon mouth. The boy went down but Sanderson had no way of knowing whether he had been hit or not. And then he stopped worrying about Ralston, for some twenty riders burst into the lower yard as if they had been fired from a cannon, yelling as they came.

He ducked as bullets hammered against the bunkhouse wall. But the attackers were training most of their fire on the door, hoping to keep the crew bottled up inside.

Ducking as low as he could, Sanderson ran for the shelter of the shed which housed the blacksmith's forge and anvil, and made it despite the bullets peppering the dust about him.

He swung around the corner of the shed, bringing up his rifle and snapping off a shot at a horseman who dashed into view. The horse stumbled and went down. The man landed on his knees, struggled to his feet and started for the timber.

Sanderson's second shot dropped him. Shots were coming steadily from the shelf. Evidently Boone Ralston had not been hit, or if so, not badly enough to take him out of the fight. And now a rifle began to speak from one of the windows of the ranch house as Ellen Jenner took a hand.

The yard was in turmoil as riders raced back and forth between the buildings. Someone with a torch was busy below the two small stacks of wild hay beside the creek. The corral gates had been flung open and a man dashed in, shouting and whirling a rope, trying to spook the frightened horses into a stampede.

They circled, heading around for the open gate. Sanderson threw a shot at the man inside the corral and saw him go down. Then he ran for the gate, trying to reach it before the bolting horses gained the open.

He heard a yell behind him and swung about to see a rider thundering down upon him. A bullet cut through the shoulder of his shirt. He fired in return, seeing the horse rear and swerve as it was hit, hurling the rider to the ground. The man rolled once and came up to his feet, jumping at Sanderson, a knife glinting in his hand.

Sanderson used the rifle barrel as a club, slashing it along the side of the attacker's head. The man dropped. Sanderson swung back toward the corral, but he was too late. The horses were already milling through the gate, scattering across the yard in all directions, adding to the confusion.

Two of the lower sheds and the stacks had caught fire. The leaping flames highlighted the yard.

Sanderson swung to snap a shot after four riders charging the main house, but a click told him the gun was empty. He dropped it, pulling his heavy Colt, running forward. He passed Ford Patton, down on one knee, firing steadily toward the lower corner of the yard. He saw Boone Ralston to the right, running in toward the house, and wondered how the boy had managed to get off the shelf so fast.

And then, suddenly, the raiders were gone, charging out of the canyon, and the crew was running for the bunkhouse to put out the fire on its roof.

Ellen Jenner came across the porch of the main house, carrying a rifle. Patton went unhurriedly to meet her, joined a moment later by Al Craig, and the night seemed very still after the hammer of the gunfire.

Only the flames hissing through the dry timbers, and the crew calling back and forth to each other, broke the night. Sanderson motioned a man toward him and together they went after a horse which had circled the main house, trapped him against the rock face and got a rope on him.

Sanderson told the man, whose name he did not remember, to saddle, to round up as many of the scattered animals as he could find. Then he walked to where the girl stood between Craig and the old foreman.

They had lost two men and had two wounded. The raiders had paid heavily, four dead and two wounded. The wounded were brought up to the ranch house and as soon as some of the horses had been gathered Sanderson sent one of the men to Massacre for the doctor. Afterward he, Patton and the girl stood on the porch, watching the fires die.

They had saved the bunkhouse, but the sheds had gone and the two haystacks were smoldering. In the fading light from the fires Ellen Jenner's young face was a grim mask.

"As soon as you get the horses up," she said, "take every man that can still ride and burn the Box P."

"Wait a minute," Sanderson said. "Isn't there any law in this valley?"

"Law? The sheriff lives at Fairview. He never comes up this way when he can help it, and when he does he takes orders from the Colonel who elected him. Bert Oxford is a special deputy as well as town marshal of Massacre, but he never does anything outside of town — and besides, he would side with Peters against us."

"But to burn the ranch?"

She indicated the still smoldering buildings with a violent slash of her hand. "What were they trying to do to us?"

He could not argue. He could even share her anger, although he had the deep conviction that most of this trouble was her own fault.

But even there he could not be sure. In his riding across the land Sanderson had known more than one big rancher who regarded his neighbors as varmints who had to be wiped out, and judging by his arrogance Colonel Peters could well be such a man.

Grazing led naturally to just such battles, for as a man's herds multiplied, so did his need for land and water. Once it had not mattered. When Peters and the original Ralston had driven their footsore Texas cattle into this valley the buffalo were nearly gone and the only human inhabitants had been a few ill-fed Indians.

But as more people drifted westward the

pressures of increasing population had collided head on with the expanding Peters empire, and what had happened here tonight was a typical result.

Greed was partly responsible, but it ran deeper than even greed, for in this business a man seemed to have to grow or die. The small outfits starved out automatically. The country was too remote, too far from the railroad to make the running of only a few head profitable.

The girl said, "Wait until I get my hat."

Sanderson started. "You're not going with us?"

She faced him squarely. "And why not? I wouldn't miss seeing the Box P go up in smoke for all the cattle in Colorado." She vanished into the house and Sanderson sensed that Patton was watching him.

He swung around to look out over the yard. Four men were mounted now, rounding up the rest of the horses, driving them across to the corral.

Fortunately few of the frightened animals had burst out of the canyon's mouth into the valley below. Instead they had run toward the timbered rocky walls which rose like a fence all around the home ranch.

Ellen Jenner came back, shrugging into a coat.

"You'd better get your coats," she said. "It's a long cold ride over there."

Sanderson nodded and moved off toward the bunkhouse with Patton at his side. The old foreman's voice was dry. "You don't like the idea, do you, mister?"

"It calls for some thought, all right."

"No," Patton said. "If we're ever going to do it the time is now. They won't be looking for an attack tonight. They were pretty well chewed up here, and they'll be dog tired. If we're lucky, we'll be in there and have our guns on them before anyone opens an eye."

Eight

Val Peters had chosen to build his home buildings on a small rise where he had a good view of the southern third of the valley's rolling floor. The moon was already down, but its reflection still carried in the sky to give Sanderson a faint picture of the pretentious buildings.

Long ago Peters had replaced his original log structure with a big house of sawed lumber, and the corrals and sheds covered a good two acres.

They reached the turn-off from the road and started toward the long, winding lane. The creek, which they had followed southward from below the town, twisted back and forth across the rich bottom land like a well filled, slow moving snake, its waters reflecting the lighter sky so that they looked silvered.

Since both the girl and Patton knew the layout and Sanderson did not, he offered no objection as they gave the orders. Patton split the riders into four groups, one under Boone Ralston to make for the corral, one under himself to pen the men in the bunkhouse, one under Sanderson to head directly for the main house and take the Colonel and Dred Stover prisoner.

The rest he told to wait with the girl at the lower edge of the yard, to ride to help any of the others who ran into trouble. There was no sign of life as they split, each bunch riding in from a different angle. Apparently there was not even a dog, and Sanderson breathed deeply with relief.

He had no real plan, but he hoped that if he could capture the Colonel, if they could take the crew without a gunfight, he might be able to get Peters and Ellen Jenner together and prove to both of them that a truce would be best for all.

They rode in silently, letting their horses walk the last two hundred feet to the house, stepping down and mounting the three stairs to the gallery.

Craig held the horses and four men trailed Sanderson as he pushed open the front door and stepped into the dark hallway. He had no idea where Peters slept and he risked a match to reveal the long expanse of corridor leading backward to the rear, with room doors opening off of it on both sides.

Stover was on the right, the third from the front. The Colonel was at the rear, on the left. Both roused to find themselves staring into the barrels of drawn guns, into the faces of angry men, and were herded ahead of their captors down the hallway and into the front room.

From outside there was a sudden burst of firing and Sanderson ran to the house door. Apparently the Box P crew had roused and were firing from the bunkhouse windows. But as far as he could see they were hemmed in by a circle of his men, screened behind the other sheds so that every time one of the defenders appeared at a door or window he was driven back by a burst of shots.

Sanderson returned to the front room. One of his men had lighted a lamp. The Colonel and Stover sat glaring at their guards and Al Craig was openly baiting the old man.

"So this is the end of the line, old man? You cast a big shadow around here, but the only one you'll make now is dangling at the end of a rope."

Val Peters wore a long flannel nightshirt which stretched to his bony ankles. His face under its windburn had a pallor like death and Sanderson feared that the man might have a heart attack.

Stover sat beyond his boss. His broken arm was splinted and bound to his side, rigidly. He growled, "Stop yapping like a coyote. The Colonel's run this valley for years and he's still running it. Laugh while you can. You'll never laugh again after we catch up with you."

Craig glanced toward Sanderson. "They make a lot of noise for a couple of whipped dogs. Shall I knock his teeth down his throat?"

"Go get Ellen."

The man stared at him for a moment, then grunted and left the house. Sanderson pulled out a chair and sat down. Both prisoners watched him in sullen silence as if recognizing that he and not Craig would decide what was to be done with them.

He said quietly, "Your crew's penned in the bunkhouse, Colonel. They haven't a chance to get out alive. You aren't as smart as I figured. You should have realized that Ellen Jenner wouldn't take another attack lying down. You should have kept watch."

Stover swore. The Colonel said nothing. The old man could bluster with the rest of them, but he also knew when to keep quiet.

Sanderson glanced at the three Jenner riders who were watching every move the prisoners made.

"You haven't got many friends tonight, Colonel. Boone Ralston would love to see you die. So would Ellen Jenner and Ford Patton, to say nothing of most of the men who rode out of the brush to help Ellen."

"Get on with it," Peters said.

"So they're fixing to burn the ranch, old man."

He saw a spasm of emotion pass across the seamed face and knew that the threat to the ranch meant far more to Peters than any threat of bodily harm to himself.

"Don't you think it's about time someone brought a little sense to this valley?"

"What's your price, drifter? How much for the rest of these men?" Peters looked at the guards, sizing them up at a single glance. "I'll give you each a thousand dollars to throw in with me. We can hold this house, and as soon as the Jenner woman walks in we can grab her."

Sanderson saw the sudden hunger in the three bearded faces. To each one of them a thousand dollars meant riches far beyond their wildest dreams. It represented nearly three years' wages, and their loyalty to Ellen Jenner was thin indeed.

His voice tightened. "I don't like you, Colonel. I don't even know why I mind seeing you burned out. I should walk away from here and let the girl do what she wants — which probably means hanging you — but I'm going to make one try. Let's draw a line across the valley, say through Massacre. Everything south of that line is your range. North of it to be split between Ellen Jenner and the Ralstons."

"I like the way you give away my range." Ellen Jenner was standing in the doorway. Behind her Sanderson had a glimpse of Al Craig, Patton and Boone Ralston.

They came in, and the girl walked over to stand before Peters. The leather quirt which seemed almost a part of her dangled from her wrist, and a tiny smile, deceptively sweet, curved her soft mouth.

"So, Colonel, we come to the end of the road. Your crew just gave up. The boys disarmed them, gave each a horse and told them to get out of the country. If any of them are caught along the Massacre, they hang. And you'll hang tonight unless you give me a bill of sale for every Box P critter in the valley."

If the old man had been pale before his

face was now waxlike. "You've gone out of your mind," he wheezed.

She shook her head. "It's you that went out of your mind. You should have finished the job at the Diamond J tonight. You must know it's one or the other of us from now on. Burning your buildings won't finish it, although that's exactly what I'm going to do. The lower sheds are already afire."

Peters made a strangled sound in his throat. He struggled to his feet, ignoring the guns and pushing his way toward the window, peering out as if he could not believe the story his eyes were telling him.

He turned back to face her, looking curiously shrunken as if his slim body had lost half its weight. "The ranch." He wasn't talking to anyone. "The ranch, it took fifty years to build."

"And fifteen minutes to destroy," Ellen Jenner said. "Come on, old man, write out that bill of sale or hang."

He slumped beside the table and sat hunched, unseeing. Sanderson was fascinated. This couldn't be happening. Yet there the girl stood, coolly taking over one of the largest ranches in this part of the country.

Incredibly he watched the Colonel reach

into a drawer, find pen and paper and write slowly in a cramped hand which showed that he was much more familiar with a gun than with a pen.

When he had finished he shoved the paper across the table. Ellen Jenner picked it up, read it twice, then shoved it to Stover.

"Witness it."

The bull-necked foreman indicated his broken arm. "I can't write."

"With your left hand."

Dred Stover glanced at the Colonel. The old man bowed his head as if he were thoroughly whipped and with an angry grunt the foreman took up the pen and awkwardly scrawled his name.

The girl turned to Sanderson.

"Sorry," he said. "I want no part of this."

She examined him with hot eyes and the quirt at her wrist jerked suggestively as if she would strike him across the face. Then with a shrug she handed the paper first to Patton, then to Boone Ralston.

The boy read it slowly, glancing at Sanderson from the corner of his eyes.

"Don't forget this man murdered your father," Ellen Jenner said. "If you ever want your ranch back, sign."

He signed carefully. She snatched the Bill of Sale from under his hand and thrust it at Patton.

"Ride to Fairview and file this at the courthouse," she said.

The old foreman nodded, folding the paper and stuffing it into the front of his shirt.

Sanderson spoke to her in a low voice, "You know you won't get away with this."

"Why not?"

"He'll never honor that Bill of Sale. You aren't settling trouble, you're just building it."

"I think not." She motioned to Al Craig and the man followed her to the door. He came back a few minutes later and nodded to the Colonel and Stover.

"Okay, you two, get dressed." He sent one of the guards to follow each man.

"Where are you taking us?" Stover said.

Craig grinned at him. "Over to the Diamond J. We'll keep you there a few days until we can shift the cattle and vent the brands. Then you'll go free."

No one in the room believed him. "You damn murderer," Stover said. The Colonel seemed to be beyond speech.

Craig took two cat-like steps forward and hit the man hard across the mouth, knocking him backward into the table's edge.

"Watch yourself. The next time I'll use a gun."

Sanderson walked out of the room. He came to the porch and found Ellen Jenner enjoying the spectacle of the burning sheds. She heard him and looked up.

"I don't believe you like working for me," she said.

He said, "A number of things happened here tonight that I didn't like."

She reached in the pocket of her coat and brought out two gold pieces.

"That should pay you for your time. Get your horse and ride out. Keep riding. I don't want to see you in the valley again."

"Keep the money," he said.

"You're a fool, Sanderson. Do you know what you're walking away from?"

"The same thing you promised Al Boston and probably Boone Ralston."

He saw her hand tighten on the loaded handle of the quirt. She flicked it upward, aiming for his eyes, but he was too quick. His hand caught the swinging thong and he jerked on it hard. The handle loop was about her wrist and he nearly pulled her from her feet as she stumbled forward into him. She steadied herself for an instant and then tried to strike his face with her free hand.

He caught her wrist, twisting it cruelly, ignoring the half-smothered moan of pain which escaped her lips. "Don't make me forget you're a woman," he said and shoved her away from him and went down the steps to the hard-baked yard.

The sheds were burning brightly now. So was the bunkhouse. He found his horse. The eastern sky looked cherry red through the billowing smoke. No one paid any attention to him. The crew was occupied tearing down the corral fence, firing the three stacks of river hay.

He mounted and rode slowly between the burning structures. At the limit of the yard he looked back in time to see Al Craig march his prisoners from the house. Then one of the riders dashed oil across the dry porch and flung a match into it, and the flames licked up to destroy the palace which Peters had constructed for himself.

Then Sanderson turned and kneed his horse forward, not following the lane but rather the curve of the looping river.

Nine

From his concealment in the brush along the valley bench, Sanderson watched the four men ride toward him. He had been watching them for a full hour, managing to stay ahead of them as they moved southward along the western edge of the valley.

Apparently they were heading for the Diamond J, keeping westward to avoid the town of Massacre, and so far neither Craig nor the rider with him had made any move to harm the prisoners.

But now they pulled up at the mouth of a small draw a good two thousand yards from where Sanderson waited in the timber. He could not hear what was said, but Craig's actions were plain enough. Craig dismounted and walked to where Stover sat his saddle, his good arm tied to the horn, and started to loosen the man's bounds.

Sanderson shifted his horse, riding slowly, carefully along the crest of the bench above the men. He was in time to hear Craig say, "All right, you two, walk up that draw. They'll never find your bodies in a million years." He saw Stover turn furiously on Craig, saw the man knock the foreman to the ground so that he fell on his broken arm. Then Craig drew his gun.

Sanderson had his rifle free of its boot, and the crash of his shot echoed from the rocks at his back.

He did not shoot to hit Craig, but so the bullet struck the ground ten yards to the left. Craig swung around. The man with him, who had not dismounted, was staring at the timber, trying to figure which direction the shot had come from. Sanderson swung down, looping the reins over the snub branch of an aspen. He fired again, ran a few feet to one side, fired, ran again and paused to empty his rifle. Then drawing the sixgun he emptied it as rapidly as he could.

It was too much for the mounted man. He cut his horse around and away, straight across the valley floor. Craig shouted something after him, then ran to his own horse and swung up. He was pivoting, bringing his gun down on the Colonel, when Sanderson raised his reloaded rifle and put a bullet through his shoulder.

Craig dropped his gun and swayed in the

saddle. The frightened horse bolted after the first fleeing rider. Sanderson cursed under his breath. He had hoped to take Craig here. He ran back to his horse, catching his boot heel in a twisted root in his haste and falling headlong.

By the time he was in the saddle, Craig and the other man had disappeared over a small rise a quarter of a mile away.

He rode out slowly. The Colonel was bending over Stover, trying to help his foreman to his feet. Their horses had spooked at the shots, drifting away to stand uncertainly, reins dragging, a hundred feet away.

The Colonel heard Sanderson coming and straightened. The gun Craig had dropped looked large in his old hand. He recognized Sanderson, and surprise held him unmoving for a moment.

Sanderson rested his rifle on his saddle-horn. He said, "Let it slide, Colonel."

Peters lowered his hand so that the gun pointed at the ground, but he did not drop it. His eyes, still as bright and fierce as those of a tired eagle, searched Sanderson's face.

"It was you shooting at them. Why?"

"I guess I just don't like murder," Sanderson said.

"But why take the trouble to save us? You don't like me either."

Sanderson thought about that. "Colonel," he said. "I don't like anything you stand for, but a man has to live with himself. I joined Ellen Jenner for reasons of my own, and if I'd let them shoot you down like a dog I'd remember it a long time." He turned his horse and rode out to round up their straying mounts, getting down and helping to boost Stover into the saddle. "From here you're on your own, you two."

"Wait a minute," Peters said. "That offer I made at the ranch — I'll double it. I need a man now that Dred is laid up."

"Aren't you forgetting something? You haven't got a ranch. Your buildings are gone, your cattle sold."

The old man snorted. "I'm alive, ain't I? No one ever pulled anything on Val Peters and got away with it. Wait until I get to Fairview. Wait until I get to the sheriff."

Sanderson said, "Your business," and walked to his horse, lifting himself into the saddle.

The old man squinted after him. "I don't understand you." His voice thinned out, complaining at this attitude which he failed to comprehend.

"No, I guess you don't." Sanderson

pulled his horse around and rode after Al Craig. If he could catch up with the wounded man now, he'd take him, no matter how many of the Diamond J crew were with him.

But he did not catch Craig. He lost the trail at the road and came into Massacre, thinking that the man probably had headed for the doctor's office.

He hadn't. He had not come into town, but everyone else in the valley seemed to be gathered there, buzzing like a hive of disturbed bees.

The sidewalks were well filled and half a hundred ponies lined the racks as he rode slowly down the street. Then a voice came out of the crowd, sharp and angry.

"There's one of them now."

He glanced around and recognized a squat man who had been with the Colonel on the preceding day, and guessed that the Box P riders who had been driven from the ranch had come into Massacre to rearm themselves.

He had ridden into a hornets' nest. He gave no sign that he had heard, but continued on down the street to pull into the rail before Mary Ralston's restaurant.

The people on the sidewalk stood a little aside for him to pass as if they feared that in some way they might be associated with him.

He came into the restaurant to find the counter full, but in a matter of half a dozen minutes every stool was empty. I sure am bad for business, he thought.

The girl had not looked in his direction after her first startled glance as he came in. Now she gathered up an armful of dirty dishes and vanished into the kitchen. He sat down in the cleared space and waited. She did not come back.

After several minutes he rose and walked around the end of the counter to the kitchen door. She was at the sink, washing dishes. She did not turn even though she must have heard his footsteps.

"Can a hungry man get something to eat?"

"Not here, you can't."

He came into the scrubbed room and stood behind her. "This is a public eating place. You have no right to refuse."

She swung to face him then, her dark eyes blazing. "Right? Right? Who are you to talk about rights? Haven't you done enough to this valley already? Get out!"

"I've done enough? What is it I'm supposed to have done?"

"Stop quibbling. You led those men to

the Peters ranch. You burned it. You kidnapped the Colonel and Stover."

"And just where did you get all this information?"

"Get it? Everybody in town knows it. Most of the Box P crew drifted in here after daylight. They've been hanging around ever since."

"What makes you think I kidnapped Peters?"

"One of the men hid under the creek bank. He saw you ride away with Peters as a prisoner."

It was a natural enough mistake. The Colonel's crew had known him as the leader of the group that had invaded the main ranch house to take the owner prisoner. On the other hand, they didn't know he had saved Peters from death. Probably they would learn of that eventually, but right now it did Sanderson no good whatever.

He said, "Would it change things if I denied that I rode out with Peters?"

She shook her head.

"I am a little surprised at your concern for Peters's and Stover's welfare."

"I have no concern," she said furiously. "I'd be less than human if I did not wish both of them dead."

"Then why are you censuring me?"

She faced him fully, and now her voice was cold with contempt. "You can't understand, can you, Mr. Sanderson? To you, this valley is merely another hole between two hills. To me, it is home, the only home I've ever known.

"What does a war here mean to you? Nothing except a chance to sell your gun. But between you and Ellen Jenner you've lighted a fuse which may blow up this whole country. I liked you, I trusted you, and you promised to try and get Boone to go with you. Thirty minutes later I saw you ride down the street with my brother following you like a faithful dog. What did Ellen Jenner promise you to make you change your mind? Was it money, or was it what she's been promising men for years? It probably was, and I can tell you now that you have very little chance to collect. She's as cold as an uncaught fish."

He laughed suddenly. He could not help it. The description was so very apt. "You're wonderful," he said.

That statement jarred her. She took a deep breath. "What are you talking about?"

"No one else in the world would ever think of describing Ellen Jenner as an uncaught fish."

She wet her lips. "Where's my brother?"

"At the Diamond J, I suppose. Or somewhere out on the range helping to round up Peters's cattle."

"The fools. Don't they know the Box P crew are rearming? Don't they know the sheriff will come from Fairview with as many deputies as he can pin a badge on? I've got to get Boone out of the country. I've got to."

"I'll find him," he said. "I'll get him away."

"You told me that once and I believed you. I won't believe you again." She caught up her shawl and started to leave the kitchen. At the door she stopped.

"Help yourself to anything you want to eat." She swept out, leaving him to stare after her. He turned slowly toward the stove. There was a pot of stew shoved far back under the heating oven.

He got a plate, served himself, poured coffee, found bread and butter and sat down at the kitchen table. He was half through the meal when he heard the restaurant front door open. He got up to peer through the serving slot in the dividing wall.

Bert Oxford had come into the restaurant. Oxford paused, looking around. Beyond him, Sanderson had a view of a crowd on the sidewalk.

He called, "Back here, marshal," and Oxford came toward the kitchen door.

Sanderson returned to his place at the table and was drinking coffee when Oxford appeared.

"Where's Mary Ralston?" Oxford asked.

"She left ten minutes ago."

Oxford shoved his hat far back on his greying head. "I'll say this for you. You're taking it pretty calmly."

Sanderson set his coffee cup on the table top. "Taking what calmly?"

The marshal's surface stolidity cracked wide open. "My god, man, don't you know there's a mob forming out on the walk? There are all kinds of rumors floating around — that you killed the Colonel and hid his body in the hills, that you hung him, that he's a prisoner at the Diamond J."

"None of which is true." Sanderson loaded his fork with the last of the stew and transferred it to his mouth.

Oxford said, "Can you prove that?"

"Peters will prove it himself in time. He's ridden for Fairview. If you doubt my word send a man to the county seat."

"You don't understand," Oxford said. "I

told you there's a mob forming outside and I meant just that. Most of Peters's crew is drunk and a lot of the people in Massacre who sympathize with them are drunk, and they've made up their minds to hang you. They're just building up their courage."

"What are you doing here?"

Oxford wet his lips, showing his nervousness. "You're under arrest for killing Peters, for burning his ranch. I'll take that gun," he added, and his own gun suddenly appeared in his hand. "I told you to keep your fight out of my town."

Sanderson did not move. "You'd better talk to Ellen Jenner about that. I've got very little to do with it."

"You joined her crew. You're her foreman."

"I was for a few hours. I'm not any more."

Oxford sounded baffled. "That doesn't make any sense. You were at the Box P this morning. Half a dozen men saw you."

"Did they also see me when I quit?"

"They didn't. Give me that gun."

Sanderson said levelly, "I have no intention of giving you my gun. I'd be a fool to do that if what you say about the mob is true. Oh, you'd probably try and protect me, but I'd rather depend on myself."

Oxford took half a step forward. "I'm not going to tell you again. Get your hands on the table before I buffalo you."

A faint smile curved Sanderson's lips but his grey green eyes were as frosty as a snowbank. "You talk too much, marshal. Clobber them first, talk later. You can shoot me because your gun is already in your hand, but I'll bet you money that I can draw mine even after I'm hit and kill you. As for buffaloing me, try swinging your gun up and I'll kill you before you hit me."

They watched each other with full attention. Perhaps five feet separated them and on the face of it Bert Oxford had a distinct advantage. He had a gun in his hand. He stood while Sanderson sat, his back to the table.

But something made the marshal hesitate.

Bert Oxford was not a coward, nor was he a fool. He had faced a number of gunfighters during the years he had worn the star, but never in his experience had he faced anyone quite like Sanderson.

The man either had nerves of steel, or no nerves at all. The mob gathering in the street outside was enough to unsettle anybody, but for all the sign Sanderson showed, the nearest mob might as well have been in the New York stock exchange.

"It's your move, marshal."

It was Bert Oxford who cracked — Bert Oxford who knew that he was growing old, who no longer could count on the fast reflexes he had been so sure of twenty years before.

"Keep your gun," he said savagely. "Turn the town into a shooting gallery. Kill half a dozen people and get yourself killed in the process." He turned angrily on his heel and stalked out of the kitchen. When he opened the outer door Sanderson could hear the voice of the mob, a swelling, bickering shrillness, no word distinguishable, but more threatening than any shout.

Ten

Sanderson sat at the table, thinking it over. There was the rear door, of course, but undoubtedly part of the crowd would be waiting in the alley to make sure he did not escape.

If he used the kitchen door the chances were that someone would shoot as soon as he appeared. If he walked out the front way they might wait to see what he intended to do.

Also, he had hitched his horse out front. He picked up his hat and set it on his head, shrugged into his coat, made sure the gun was free in the holster by lifting it halfway and then sliding it back into place.

Afterward he walked into the dining room and crossed it slowly toward the front door. He could see them on the sidewalk outside and judged that there must be twenty men. As he advanced they retreated to form a half circle around the entrance. No one wanted to get caught too close to the swinging door.

He thrust it open, and stepped out onto the boards of the sidewalk, letting his level, intent gaze range slowly around the circle as if he were trying to memorize every face.

At once he sensed something important. They had no leader. For years they had followed the Colonel and Stover, letting the ranch owner and foreman do their thinking until the habit of obedience had become the pattern of their lives.

They didn't fear him. They just needed someone to open the attack.

But also this leaderlessness could work against him. He knew from experience that the best way to break a mob was to single out the leader, to keep a steady pressure on him, to force him to back down if possible.

Since there was no leader he chose one, a tall man standing midway in the semicircle, directly before that part of the rack at which Sanderson's horse was tethered.

Sanderson had no idea what the man's name was, nor did he care. But he took a step forward, a measured step, his hand close to his gun, not touching it, but making his intent plain.

"Shorty," he said, "turn around and untie my horse."

The man's eyes rolled with surprise, and he turned his head a little, one way and then the other, trying to decide who Sanderson was talking to.

"I'm talking to you," Sanderson said. "Turn around and untie that horse." He took another measured step forward.

This was the problem. He could not advance too far or the men who were now on his flanks would be behind him. It was a desperate gamble, one he probably would not win, but he had to play the hand out now.

Still the tall fellow hesitated. He looked worriedly at the men on either side of him.

"I can kill you so easy," Sanderson said. "I can empty my iron before they can even clear leather."

His gun was suddenly in his hand. They had been watching his face as he talked and the speed with which the gun had appeared sobered all of them.

They stood there, momentarily robbed of will.

"Untie that horse," Sanderson said.

The tall man turned slowly, his hand going to the knotted reins, and a kind of sigh ran through the group, exhaling its pentup breath.

For the first time since leaving the doorway Sanderson let his eyes range above their heads. There were people on the opposite walk, people all along the street, watching, townspeople who had taken no part in this action and apparently wanted none.

He guessed that most of Massacre's citizens would take no part. Few of them had any love for Peters or the Box P, but by a like token, he was a stranger to them and they would not raise a finger to come to his aid.

He wasted a second scanning the street, then brought his full attention back to the men before him. The tall one was still fumbling with the reins. The others stood watchful, waiting for a break. He could not hold them long. Time was against him.

"All right," he said. "All of you except Shorty move over to my right. Easy now. One at a time. And get your hands in the air."

The hands came up slowly, one after another. He held his breath. Any one of the twenty men might choose this moment to try for his gun.

None did. With hands raised they shifted until all of them were on his right. At his order they turned and faced the building.

He still had the problem of getting on his horse, of holding them until he could swing the animal and ride out. And then he saw Mary Ralston coming down the street from the livery, riding a dun horse, a rifle across her saddle. She pulled up to the rack.

"I'll cover them," she said. "Get their guns."

He grinned then, partly from relief, partly at the grim resolution on her face.

"Good girl." He moved down the line, slowly, careful not to step between her and a man in the line until he had disarmed him. The guns he broke, emptying the shells into his palm and dropping these into his coat pocket. The guns he tossed into the dust of the street.

When the last gun had been thrown away he retreated to his horse, ducking under the rack and swinging up into the saddle.

"Let's go," he said.

They rode neck and neck for the edge of town, past the watching townspeople, past the hotel corner. Sanderson saw Bert Oxford on the hotel gallery and knew that the old marshal had watched the happenings before the restaurant from a safe distance.

They clattered over the small bridge. The girl swung out of the road, into a faint trail that headed toward the valley's bench. Sanderson followed without question, and she ran her horse a good mile before pulling in to let the animal blow.

"You're a fool," she said as he drew up at her side.

He lifted an eyebrow, looking at her quizzically. "There's certainly no argument about that. But what specific act are you talking about at the moment?"

"To walk out of the restaurant. To try and face all those men alone."

"And just what else could I have done?"

"At least if you'd stayed inside you could have picked them off, one by one."

He shook his head. "They'd have gotten me sooner or later. Once the shooting started I wouldn't have stood a chance of coming out alive. I probably wouldn't have made it if you hadn't shown up. I caught them unready when I walked out. They didn't have a leader and they didn't have a plan. But I couldn't have disarmed them alone. Or even if I did, the minute I hit the saddle they would have swung around, shooting."

She didn't answer. She was looking at their back trail. So far there was no sign of pursuit.

"What made you come to help me?" he asked.

She shook her head as if she herself did

not quite know the answer. "When I rode out of the livery it was the last thing I had in mind. I figured you were getting exactly what you deserved, what you'd earned. But I couldn't leave anybody to face a mob like that alone. No decent person could."

"A number of people in Massacre were doing exactly that," he said dryly, "including the marshal."

She gestured vaguely, having no words to convey the way she felt about her neighbors' actions. "If you're smart, you'll head directly for the timber and make your way out of the valley as soon as you can."

"What about you?"

"I'm going to find my brother and get him away too."

"I'll help you. I'm not going to leave you riding around alone — not with the type of men who are going to be roaming this country in the next few days."

"I can take care of myself, Sanderson."

He merely smiled as he took a long look at their back trail. There was still no sign of pursuit. Certainly if the Box P crew meant to follow them they would have started by now.

She touched her horse with the spur and rode on, Sanderson following, still heading for the green line the timber made as it ran down the side of the high bench. But instead of heading into it she angled off to the north, paralleling the hills, not glancing back, ignoring him.

He watched her speculatively, noting the ease with which she rode, the way she sat the saddle, her lithe body seeming to be almost a part of the horse.

At four o'clock they topped a small rise and he saw the lone chimney standing like a stark lonely sentinel above the charred timbers of the burned house.

Mary Ralston checked her horse and sat for a long time, gazing down at her former home. Sanderson made no effort to intrude. At last she urged her horse forward. Riding slowly past the sink, past the dead cattle her brother had shot, she went on toward the Diamond J.

Activity in the ranch yard ceased as they rode up. The crew gathered into a tight knot, close to the corral, watching them come.

Sanderson noted that most of the men carried rifles and realized that Ellen Jenner was taking no chances. Al Craig probably had brought the word of the Colonel's and Stover's escape.

They rode in close, and Ellen Jenner appeared on the porch of the main house, Al

Craig and Boone Ralston behind her. She stopped suddenly, surprise pinching her face, but Boone Ralston came down the steps and across the hard yard to meet them.

"Sis, what are you doing here?"

She swung down, tossing her reins to Sanderson.

"I want to talk to you, Boone. Alone."

He hesitated, the sullenness which Sanderson had learned to know so well making his face ugly. "There's nothing to talk about."

"Then why are you afraid to talk with me?"

"I'm not afraid," he growled.

She led him away from the group, and Sanderson could see them in heated argument. Then Ellen Jenner came forward with Al Craig.

"Why did you come back?" she asked.

"Miss Ralston wanted to talk with her brother. I rode along for company."

She hesitated over the next question. "Where — where did you run into her?"

"Massacre."

"Did you? Were Colonel Peters and Stover in town?"

He could have pretended surprise. He could have said he did not know that Peters and Stover were free. He didn't. He kept an eye on Al Craig, whose good hand hung close to his holstered gun.

"They weren't in town," he said, "but most of the crew was."

"I'm surprised you didn't have trouble."

He allowed himself a small smile. "There was some talk of hanging me. They changed their minds."

He saw her eyes flash with interest. Then they dulled as Mary Ralston came again toward them, trailed by her obviously un-willing brother.

"A word with you, Ellen."

Mary Ralston was shorter and slighter than the other girl, but she stood straight and proud, and Sanderson realized that she did not suffer by comparison.

"I'm taking my brother away," Mary said.

"Are you?" Ellen purred. "Now isn't that nice. What's the matter — afraid he'll be contaminated by associating with my men?"

"Because he'll be killed if I don't." There was a flat quality in the statement that could not be met by argument. "You're a fool, Ellen. You were lucky. Peters let you alone because you weren't like us, because you had very little that he actually wanted.

But you had to make this fight, and I don't feel sorry about what's going to happen to you."

"And what is going to happen to me?"

"You burned his ranch, but his crew is still alive. So is Peters. Before this day is out there'll be men riding here from Massacre and other men from Fairview. The sheriff for one. Can't you see that what you did played directly into the Colonel's hands? When you burned his place you put yourself outside the law."

There was cold fury in Ellen Jenner as she pointed to her charred sheds. "Who started the burning?"

"Who started the war?" Mary countered, and they looked at each other with deep anger, two people who could never be friends even though they equally hated the same man. Then Mary Ralston turned away, moving around Sanderson.

"Get your horse, Boone," she said over her shoulder. Sanderson glanced at the watching crew. He could sense a change in their mood. They had overheard everything Mary had said and now they were silently questioning each other.

Boone Ralston stood undecided as his sister lifted herself into her saddle. Sanderson spoke gently.

"Get your horse, Boone. Hasn't your sister been hurt enough?"

"Oh, god," Boone Ralston said. "Are you scared too?"

"He's so scared," Mary said, "that he backed down the Box P crew single handed. Listen to him, Boone, even if you won't listen to me."

"All right." The words seemed to be torn out of the boy. "All right. I hate to run like a dog, but if it will make you happy I'll get my horse."

"Stay where you are." Ellen Jenner's voice cracked as if she had snapped the quirt she still carried. "You're in this deal, Boone, and you're going to stay in. No one leaves." She turned, her eyes sweeping her crew. "No one, not even you, Mr. Sanderson. Try to ride out and we'll put a bullet in your back."

Eleven

They were prisoners.

"Don't move, either of you," Al Craig said. His shoulder was bandaged but the wound did not seem to bother him. He held the gun steady. "Drop that belt, Sanderson, and be careful."

Sanderson unfastened the buckle of his gun belt and let the heavy weapon slide to the ground beside his horse. Boone Ralston also dropped his gun. Ellen came forward to jerk the rifle from Sanderson's boot and then from Mary Ralston's.

"You can step down now," she said.

They dismounted slowly. She motioned toward the porch of the ranch house. "Get over there and make yourselves comfortable."

"Wait," Al Craig said. He seemed to be running the crew. He walked to Sanderson, stiff-legged, carefully choosing a spot to place each foot before taking a step. His boldly prominent eyes searched Sanderson's face.

"There's something strange about you, Sanderson. Ellen tells me you came over the ridge."

Sanderson shrugged indifferently. "So I did," he said.

"Why?"

Sanderson said, "My business," and knew that he was in as much danger as he had ever been in his life. Craig had guessed his errand and one wrong move would bring on his death. He could see the desire to kill glowing in the man's eyes.

"I think it's mine." Craig's voice was little more than a whisper. "I came over that ridge too. I think you were following me."

Sanderson allowed his face to show comprehension and a faint surprise. "So it was your tracks I saw. I wondered what fool would try those snowbanks."

"You were following me."

"I was following your tracks. They showed the way through the pass. They broke a trail."

"You're after me." The man's face was stark with concentration, as if he were goading himself to a kind of frenzy, the frenzy he needed to turn himself into an executioner.

Sanderson said slowly, "I never saw you in my life before I saw you at the livery in

Massacre. If I were after you for something, friend, why didn't I kill you then? Why did I ride away from the Colonel's ranch without finishing you?"

He saw the flicker of indecision flash briefly and knew that he had scored. It would not occur to a man like Craig that someone following him to avenge a murder would have the self control to hold his hand, to bide his time until an arrest was possible.

He stood uncertain, rocking a little on the balls of his feet, and in that moment Sanderson's life hung by the slimmest thread. Then the moment passed.

"We'll see, we'll see," Craig muttered, and dropped his gun into leather.

The tension which had crept through Sanderson's body eased. But then he found Ellen Jenner's blue eyes upon him, mocking him. He wasn't fooling her one bit, and he knew it.

He walked to the porch between Mary and Boone Ralston and settled himself on the top step. Boone was fuming, and his resentment had turned on Ellen Jenner.

"What right has she to hold us here?"

"Stop and think, Boone," Mary said. "You know Ellen doesn't need a right to do anything she chooses."

"But what does she gain? Certainly she doesn't expect us to help her fight when we're being held against our will?"

"She couldn't let us ride away," Sanderson said. "The crew heard what Mary said. They were beginning to spook. Each one was thinking that maybe the smart thing to do was fade into the hills. By holding us she proves that she's still boss around here, and if anybody tries to pull his picket pin he's liable to get shot doing it."

The boy lapsed into silence. Mary Ralston asked quietly, "Was that man right? Were you following him? Are you some kind of an officer?"

"Would it make a difference?"

"It would explain a number of things which have been puzzling me — actions you took which didn't fit together."

"Let it pass," he said. "If Craig really thought I was after him I'd be dead."

"Craig? Is that his name?" Boone Ralston was staring at him with renewed curiosity. "I thought he was called Boston."

Sanderson cursed himself silently. It was a slip. Made in other company, it could finish him.

"Forget it," he said.

"Sure —" The boy broke off as Ellen

Jenner came away from a conference with Craig and Ford Patton and walked toward them. She halted before the steps, considering them.

"You showed no surprise when I asked if Peters and Stover were in town. You knew they were free. How did you know?"

Sanderson just sighed.

"You were the one who shot Boston from ambush, weren't you? You turned them free. Why?"

Still he did not answer. It was fruitless to tell her that he simply could not sit by and allow a cold-blooded murder. He knew Boone Ralston was staring at him dumbstruck, but he could do nothing about that either.

"What did you do?" Ellen demanded. "Make a deal with the Colonel that if he captured Boston he would turn Al over to you? You are after Boston, aren't you?"

"I made no deal with Peters," Sanderson said.

"Look, you." Her voice was harsh now. "Stop trying to play word games with me. Boston is still suspicious of you. I don't know what he did on the other side of the mountain and I don't care. But it must have been something exceptional, for him to buck those drifts at this time of the year.

And you must have wanted him pretty bad or you wouldn't have followed him."

Sanderson said nothing.

"One word from me and he'll kill you now," she said. "I think you know that."

"Uh-huh," Sanderson agreed.

"So I'm offering a trade. Help me with Peters and I won't tell Boston. I'll even help you round him up after this is over."

He almost gasped at her brazen disloyalty to everyone except herself. He guessed that even if he agreed to her terms, when the time came she would refuse to give Craig to him. But he let none of these thoughts show in his face.

"And how would you know that you could trust me — that I wouldn't ride off over the ridge?"

Her eyes flicked to Mary Ralston and back to him. "That seems simple. I'll keep Mary here. I don't think you or Boone will get out of line as long as you know she's my prisoner. I believe we understand each other, Sanderson. You realize by now that I'm no ordinary woman. Cross me and I'll shoot her as quickly as I'd shoot a coyote. Get any idea that I'm trying to bluff out of your head. I mean exactly what I say."

Boone Ralston growled deep in his throat.

"You wouldn't!"

"You're a fool, Boone." She stood there sneering at the boy. "You always were, but don't make any mistake. I'd as soon kill your sister as I would a man."

Sanderson cut her short. "What is it you want us to do?"

"Kill Peters. When I'm sure he's dead Mary can ride out anywhere she chooses as long as she leaves the valley."

Sanderson needed no one to tell him why Ellen Jenner wanted the other girl to leave the valley. Ellen Jenner wanted no ghosts from the past to rise and challenge her domination of the Massacre.

He heard Mary's sharp drawn breath, heard the shake in her voice as she said, "I won't have it. Do you think I want anyone buying my life with a murder?"

"You have no choice." Ellen Jenner sounded final. "Either they take care of Peters or I'll hang the lot of you."

"And how are we supposed to have a chance against him when he escaped your full crew?" The words burst out of Boone Ralston.

She looked at him and her smile was deadlier than if she had frowned. "That's the point, my friend. Sanderson rescued him from Al Boston. I'm as certain of that as if I'd been there. Naturally Peters won't suspect that the man who saved his life will turn around and kill him. Isn't that right, Sanderson?"

He drew in a long breath.

"It's your choice," he said.

He stood up slowly.

Mary Ralston leaped up to face him. "No!"

"I've got you into this," he said gently. "If I'd ridden out of the valley as you asked, if I'd taken your brother with me, you would not be in this situation now. I stayed for reasons of my own. So it seems to me that I'm the one who should try to correct the mistake."

"That isn't fair." She said it with fierce intensity. "I had no right to ask anything of you in the first place. You were a stranger. Our problems were not your affair. Ride away. Forget about me." She looked with utter contempt at Ellen Jenner. "Let her do what she likes. I won't have my life bought by the blood of another man."

Ellen Jenner laughed. "How bold we are." She turned to Sanderson. "You can't do business with children. Neither of these two has ever grown up. You and I face facts, don't we?"

He nodded.

"You've got one minute to make up your mind."

"It's already made up." He stepped down to the ground. "I suppose you'll let us have our guns? I'm not much good at killing people with my bare hands."

"You'll get your guns. Ford Patton will ride out with you for a mile and hand them over. I want no heroics here."

"All right."

"You'll find Peters and stop him. I warn you now that the first sign of attack, either by you or by his men, will bring on her death." She jabbed her finger at Mary and swung away and walked across the yard.

Boone Ralston was swearing under his breath. "I'll kill her. So help me, if she so much as touches Sis I'll kill her."

Sanderson had no stomach for useless argument. He looked at the silent girl for a long moment, reading the message in her eyes, knowing that she was telling him to ride away when he could, to give no thought to her. Then without even saying goodbye he followed Ellen Jenner.

Boone Ralston lingered on the steps. Sanderson could not hear what the boy said to his sister, but as he reached the horses and turned he saw Boone take Mary into his arms, saw the way she clung to him, and then Ellen's mockery jarred him.

"Touching, isn't it?"

"Doesn't anything have any value to you?"

"The valley does. Give me the valley and ask what you like."

He swung to the saddle with a feeling of hopelessness. He sat watching as Boone crossed to him and came into the saddle of his sister's horse. Then they rode out, trailed by Patton who had their guns looped over his saddle-horn, their rifles carried across his knees.

A half mile down the road to Fairview Patton called a halt. He dropped the guns into the thick grass beside the trail and spurred back toward the ranch as if he feared that they would recover the weapons and ride in pursuit.

Sanderson took his time, stepping down, lifting his own guns and then handing up Boone's. The boy fitted his belt into place sullenly while Sanderson climbed back into the saddle.

"What do we do now?" Boone asked.

"What do you suggest?"

"Damn it, for two cents I'd throw in with Peters. I never thought Ellen Jenner would act like this. Why, she's worse than the Colonel."

"And what happens to your sister?"

Boone bit his lip. "All right. You tell me."

"I will, then. First we hunt up the sheriff and tell him what's happened. You don't know it but I'm a stock detective in the employ of the Cattlemen's Association, and law officers usually cooperate with us."

"You don't know Gilpen."

"The sheriff?"

"That's right. He never had a thought in his head that wasn't put there by the Colonel."

"Maybe, but I think he'll listen to me. I'll get the sheriff and ride back to the Diamond J with him. We'll tell Ellen exactly where she stands. She might fight the Colonel, but I doubt she'd try to fight the sheriff and the power of the Cattlemen's Association. If you don't want to come to Fairview with me, all right. You head for the brush until this is over. Probably better if you did. That way you won't stand as much chance of running into Peters and his crew."

Anger made Boone Ralston's voice tight. "I'm not afraid. I'm not running from anyone."

Sanderson shrugged and wheeled his horse, taking the road toward Fairview.

They rode in silence for nearly an hour. The sun was well down behind the ridge and the timber threw long, spiked shadows far out across the valley. Then they saw the dust on the trail ahead.

At once Sanderson pulled up. The men riding toward Ellen were much too far away to distinguish, but he guessed that they could only be Peters's men, probably accompanying the sheriff.

"You'd better ride off." He turned to the boy.

"Hell with you. I'm no more afraid of Peters than you are."

"I did Peters a small favor this morning."

"So it was you that broke him free. Damn it, Sanderson, you've caused a lot of trouble in this valley with your meddling. If you hadn't turned him loose Ellen wouldn't be holding Mary a prisoner."

There was a lot of truth in what the boy said, and Sanderson knew it. His meddling might have changed the course of events in the valley. But the basic situation was not his fault.

"Stay here or ride out," he said, "but at least wait around until I talk to them."

He did not wait for an answer. He urged his horse forward at a half run.

Twelve

There were fourteen men in the party. Sanderson recognized Stover by the sling which still bound the foreman's broken arm to his side, and there was no mistaking the Colonel's slight form in its black coat and shallow crowned hat.

As they spotted him the party broke into two halves, one swinging right, one left, as if to encircle him. He drove directly through to face Stover, the Colonel and a grey haired man he had never seen before. This man wore a bronze star pinned to his shirt pocket, and Sanderson guessed him to be the sheriff, Gilpen.

The Colonel had halted his horse and sat facing Sanderson, his old nutcracker face an unreadable mask. "What are you doing here? I thought you'd be out of the country by now."

Sanderson told him in a dozen tense phrases.

The Colonel listened in silence, showing no emotion.

"Where's young Ralston?"

Sanderson moved his arm in a wide sweep, indicating the hill he had just come over. "He's waiting for my signal. He doesn't want any trouble."

"Tell him to ride in."

Sanderson turned in the saddle and waved both arms. He saw Boone Ralston on the crest of the rise, saw the boy start forward, and turned back to Peters. The sheriff and Stover had uttered not a word.

"The way I see it," he said, "if the sheriff and a couple of men will ride with me to the Diamond J we can get Miss Ralston free without harm."

"We'll see." Peters muttered something to Stover in an undertone which Sanderson did not catch, and the foreman swung his horse away to the left.

Sanderson said, "Now's the time to end the fight, Colonel. Why carry it on? What is it buying either of you?"

Peters just looked at him, his old face seeming to be carved from granite.

Boone Ralston was nervous, but being young he tried to brazen it out. He rode in glancing right and left at the riders flanking him on either side, and then with attempted lightness he said, "Well, Colonel, it looks like you and I are on the same side for once."

"Gimme that gun," Peters said.

The boy's head jerked up with surprise and his hand dropped automatically to the holstered Colts at his side. As he did so a rope hissed from his left and the loop settled around his arms, binding them tight to his sides.

Sanderson swung his horse half around, a muttered protest on his lips. He saw the second loop, tried to avoid it, and was too late. The heavy braided lariat dropped around him and jerked him from his horse. He fell heavily on his side. Before he could regain enough air to move two men leaped from their saddles, one wrenching the gun from his belt, the other pinning him down, a knee in his back.

Boone Ralston had been disarmed and his wrists bound behind him, without being lifted from the saddle.

Sanderson lay perfectly still, his face ground cruelly in the dirt by the pressure of the man on his back.

"Let him up," the Colonel said, his voice dry as a rustling husk in a wind.

The man got off of Sanderson's back. He rose to his hands and knees, still groggy from lack of air, then slowly came to his feet. His cheek had been cut by the gravel and he lifted a hand to wipe away the smear of blood.

Inside he was raging, but he hung on to his temper.

"What do you think you're trying to do?" he demanded.

"Hang a cow thief." The Colonel sounded pleased.

"Hang?" Sanderson stared up at him. "You mean the boy?"

"I mean Ralston. I warned all of them what would happen."

"But he rode in. He was offering to join you, to help you."

"When he got in trouble he rode in. He might help me now and turn on me next week." The old man's voice was inflexible. "I know the breed. You can't trust any of them."

"But you can't hang a man, not without a trial." He appealed to the sheriff. "You're a law officer. You can't just sit by and see a boy murdered."

Gilpen shifted uneasily in his saddle.

"Colonel, let's not be hasty."

"Hasty?" Peters repeated. "Hasty? Listen, you fool. These people burned me out, they made me sign a bill of sale for my cattle. Isn't that stealing? Isn't that rustling on a wholesale scale? Haven't we always hung rustlers in this country? What are you talking about?"

"But he's not much more than a boy."

"Boy is it?" The Colonel forced his horse forward until he was at Boone's side. "Do you deny that you and Ellen Jenner got together to drive me from the valley? Do you deny that you helped lead the crew that burned me out? Do you deny that you helped her force me to sign a bill of sale for my cattle?"

Boone Ralston watched him levelly. The young face under its heavy wind tan was very white, but after his first start of shock at the word "hang" he seemed to have gotten control of his nerves.

"Why deny it?" he said in a careful voice which no longer had a hint of braggadocio. "You murdered my father. Why shouldn't you murder me?"

"I don't call it murder," Peters said. "I call it justice. You knew what you were getting into when you started this. You had to know that there was only one possible ending — either your death or mine. What about the men you sent me out with this morning? Weren't they planning to kill me?"

The boy did not answer. He shifted himself a little in his seat, handicapped by his bound arms.

"Answer me."

"I'd kill you now if I had a chance," Boone Ralston said.

Peters backed his horse. "All right, take him over to the timber and find a good tree."

"Wait," Sanderson said. "Wait!"

"Shut up," the Colonel told him. "If you hadn't saved my life this morning you'd be riding with him. You took a piece of a fight which was none of your business, and you deserve to hang along with the rest. But I pay my debts. You're free to ride, but I'm warning you that if we ever see you in this valley again you'll get the same as young Ralston."

"You'd better kill me now," Sanderson said. "I'll tell you that if you hang that boy I'll hunt you down one by one, and put a rope around every neck."

Stover cursed. He drove his horse straight into Sanderson, swinging his gun with his good arm, bringing it down squarely on the crown of Sanderson's head.

Sanderson collapsed and the frightened horse jumped over him. They left him where he lay, not even giving him a second glance as they bunched around Boone Ralston, herding him forward toward the timber and his death.

Sanderson was not completely unconscious. He was aware of their going but seemed unable to raise himself or even to open his eyes.

How long he lay thus he could never afterward remember. It seemed hours, but was in reality only minutes. Slowly he lifted his body to his knees and squatted, peering around in the gathering darkness.

His horse, the reins trailing, grazed unhurriedly some fifty feet away. He rose and walked toward it, his steps unsteady, and the animal moved away from him.

He spoke sharply and it stopped, lifting its head, shying uncertainly. He caught the trailing rein and lifted himself painfully to the saddle and sat for a moment, listening to the sounds filtering across the valley.

There was still light enough to show the marks of the Colonel's party as it had cut toward the black fringe of timber along the swell of the bench, and he followed these. He had no definite purpose. He was still not thinking clearly and without a gun he was powerless to stop them. He knew too that there was no use in riding to the Diamond J for help. Help would never come in time, even if Ellen Jenner should be willing to send her crew to rescue Ralston.

He quickened his pace, awareness coming slowly back to him, fearful that he would lose the trail in the increasing darkness. Even so it was moonrise by the time he reached the first line of the trees.

The silver glow from the full sphere that swam up into the eastern sky showed him what he had dreaded to see, the long, limp body of Boone Ralston, its neck canted at a sharp angle, swaying below an outthrust branch.

His horse spooked but he forced it under the limb. Grasping the dead youth under the armpits, he cut the rope which clutched the neck and lowered the body to the ground.

He had no tools for a proper burial. He had to content himself with rocks, heaping them on the body as a protection against marauding animals.

His head began to clear. A bump had risen where Stover's gun barrel had broken the skin, but it left only a dull ache.

It never entered his mind to ride out of the valley. He could still hear Mary Ralston's pleading voice, and he knew that he would avenge the death of her brother with the last breath of his body.

It was strange, he thought. He had hated Craig for killing Martha Horn, and he had been certain of his love for that girl. Theirs had been a friendship through the years, a warm, pleasant association not marked with burning passions.

He knew now that his relationship with the dead girl had been fostered by habit and familiarity and not by any deep love. Even in his grief he had still been willing for the law to handle Craig's punishment. And in the light of this realization he reviewed his feelings for Mary Ralston.

From the first time he had walked into her restaurant he had felt the pull of her personality, even when he had expected never to see her again.

And now because of him, her brother was dead. Certainly she had suffered enough at the hands of Peters without this added blow. And aside from her grief, she was in imminent personal danger. The thought jerked him erect and sent him running to his horse.

What would happen to her at the Diamond J when Peters and his men attacked? In his concern for the dead boy, in his fuzzy mental state, he had forgotten Ellen Jenner's threat.

He mounted and spurred out of the

timber onto the open shoulder of the bench.

If the Peters crew was no more than half an hour ahead of him, he stood a chance of overtaking them before they reached the ranch. Undoubtedly they would attack the canyon from the front, and the thought came that if he could cut through the lower hills and hit the trail which led back to Crawford's he might be in time.

It was a long chance, traveling strange, rough country in the dark, but it was the only way he could possibly reach the ranch ahead of the attackers.

He swung his horse in dangerous speed along the uneven surface of the bench, staying out from the timber, counting desperately on the fact that he was heading for the Diamond J in a nearly direct line while Peters, if his crew followed the trail, must make a wide loop to eastward before coming back to the rising western hills.

He rode on doggedly. The rising moon was a pale disk high above the tree tops now, shedding an eerie light which showed him enough of the ground to make fair progress. And then he struck a rock ridge that barred his path and slanted far out across the bench.

He guessed that beyond this wall lay the

canyon of the Diamond J and halted his horse, letting the animal blow, studying the rocky tree studded slope ahead.

He could turn left and follow it around until he reached the jaw-like mouth of the canyon housing the ranch. Or he could attempt to scale the ridge and so reach the narrow, winding road between the ranch and the outlaw hideout in the hills.

He chose to go over the hump, turned the horse into the timber and began at once to climb.

In places here the trees grew so close together that their foliage made an arch shutting out any light from the distant moon.

Progress was very slow, and he knew an overriding impatience as he wound in at the head of one box canyon from which there was no egress. He turned back, tensely retracing his way to a point where the side canyon wall leveled out enough to be climbed.

Twice more he had to backtrack, but finally he reached the crest and started downward. Here the timber was heavier yet. He had to force a path between the close-growing pole pines. He toiled urgently, finally dismounting and leading the horse, until he slid down a twenty foot bank to land in a well traveled track.

He stopped. The horse was shivering from the sudden descent, snorting his displeasure at his surroundings.

Sanderson let him blow, then turned into the trace. He could not be sure, but he prayed that this was indeed the Crawford road.

He had lost all track of time, but he had heard no sound of shooting and he could only hope that the Peters crew had not yet reached the ranch.

The trail, for it was little more, looped back and forth in its descent with heart-breaking deliberateness. Then as he rounded the shoulder of a rock he saw lights glowing in the basin below him, and knew that he had reached the Diamond J.

From the rim of the yard, where the trail merged into the cover of grass, he sent out his call. Shadowy, nervous figures ran zig-zagging toward him, and he sensed the tension under which Ellen Jenner's crew faced the night.

"Who's that?" Al Craig's challenge came as the man emerged from the shadow hugging the house and halted, the moon glinting on his drawn gun.

"Sanderson."

Craig turned to speak to two men who had followed him, and they fanned out as Sanderson rode in.

"Get your hands in the air."

Sanderson held up his hands. "I haven't got a gun. Where's Ellen Jenner?"

"Here." She stood in the shadow behind Craig. "Where's your gun?"

"Peters took it."

"What are you doing, coming in that way? Where's Boone Ralston?"

"Dead." He said it in a low voice. He did not know where Mary Ralston was, and did not want her to hear the news now.

"Dead?" The suspicion thickened. "How did he die?"

"They hung him."

"Hung him? Oh, no."

The voice came from a rear window of the house, and he knew that Mary Ralston had heard his words.

Thirteen

They crowded around him.

"What happened?" Ellen Jenner demanded. "Where is Peters?"

"Coming this way. I beat them by coming through the hills."

She stood silent, thinking about that.

"The sheriff's with them," he added.

"And what made you come back?" She was still suspicious.

"Mary Ralston. It isn't her fault that we didn't stop Peters."

"How come he hung Ralston and not you?"

He had expected them to ask the question. If he admitted that Peters had spared his life because he had rescued the Colonel from Craig that morning, they would probably kill him, so he lied a little.

"I guess they thought I was dead. Stover couldn't forget that I broke his arm. Stover buffaloed me." He removed his hat and bowed his head so they could see the

179

raised welt under the hair, the dried blood matted around the wound.

Craig grunted and Ellen said, "You've got a cracked head and that's for sure." She sounded almost amused, as if it pleased her that he had suffered pain. "Now that you're here what are you going to do?"

"Give me a gun and a crack at Peters."

She studied him speculatively, then she turned to Patton. "Find him a gun and a rifle."

There was a rumble of protest from Craig. She stilled it with a motion of her hand and they stood waiting while Patton moved to the bunkhouse and came back with a rifle and an old Colt.

Sanderson took the gun, testing the weight and balance, then spun the cylinder, checked the loads and dropped it into his empty holster.

"How soon will they be here?" Patton sounded nervous. This nervousness was a poorly hidden thing which ran across the yard, affecting the full crew. The news that Boone Ralston had been hanged brought home sharply to each of the rag-tailed crew exactly what would happen to him if he chanced to fall into Peters's hands.

"They should have been here by now," Sanderson said, and turned toward the house. Ellen Jenner barred his way.

"Where are you going?"

"To see Mary Ralston. No use your holding her prisoner now."

"How do I know all this isn't a trick? How do I know that Boone Ralston isn't hiding somewhere out in the brush with your guns? How do I know that Peters is even headed this way?"

"You don't. But there comes a time when you have to trust someone, much as you dislike to."

As if in answer to his words a yell came down from a man mounted high on the lookout shelf. "Here they are!" He fired, and they whirled in time to see the shadowy riders burst through the canyon neck and flow out into the lower yard.

Ellen swore like a man. She ran to the porch where she had laid her rifle and began firing at the invaders, now moving up the open slope.

Sanderson ran past her into the house. She shouted something after him which he did not understand. He did not pause, but raced along the central hall to the door of the room at the rear from which he had heard Mary Ralston's voice.

The door was locked. He stared at the heavy planks for a moment, retreated and launched himself against them, striking the panel with the full weight of his two hundred pounds.

The lock snapped and he went headlong into the room, only regaining his balance by a miracle. There was no light, but he saw Mary faintly outlined against the far window.

"Who is it?"

"Sanderson. We've got to get out of here fast."

She said sharply, distinctly, "I'm not going anywhere with you."

"You haven't got a lot of choice," he told her in a tight voice. "Peters's men are in the yard and from the way the Diamond J crew looks I think they'll bolt." He wasted no more time in argument but moved to the window and measured the distance to the ground.

"Come on." He stepped over the sill and dropped easily to the stony earth below. The window was above the level of his head.

"Come." He extended his arms upward to catch her.

She hesitated, but a fresh burst of firing from the front of the house made her decision. She slipped one leg and then the other over the sill and dropped lightly into his arms.

His horse stood where he had left him tied to a post at the rear of the building. He led Mary forward, ignoring her protests, and lifted her into his saddle, freeing the reins.

"Head for Crawford's," he said.

Still she protested. He used his hat to fan the rump of the horse and the frightened animal leaped away toward the entrance of the rocky trail.

Then he ran back to the corner of the house, finding Ellen Jenner and Ford Patton there, firing steadily.

The bunkhouse and the cook shack were burning, their rising flames climbing into the night to add their red glow to the pale moonlight, turning the yard into an eerie stage where yelling horsemen cut back and forth like angry banshees.

Patton heard him and spun, and the firelight glinted against the old foreman's eyes. "Damn them. They're running out."

Sanderson knew what he meant. The Diamond J crew was melting away into the brush of the canyon sides. He saw Al Craig working his way back toward the porch, and a minute later the fugitive came around the shelter of the house corner, panting heavily.

"We gotta get out of here."

Sanderson had a clear view of Dred Stover as the burly foreman of the Box P spurred around the pyre of the bunkhouse. He raised his rifle and shot carefully, but saw the horse fall, saw Stover pitch over the animal's head, and knew that he had missed the man.

Craig and Patton were arguing with Ellen Jenner. She was crying, not from fear but from rage.

"I won't go. I won't. I won't."

Patton had her by the shoulders. "You've got to. We can't hold out any longer. Most of the crew have already gone."

She struggled, wailing angrily against the surging night. "Let me go. You cowards. Go ahead and run. I never will."

Craig came to Patton's aid and together they forced the still fighting girl back toward the trail. Sanderson paid them no attention. He concentrated on the figures in the fire-bright yard. His rifle spoke once, twice, a third time, and at each shot a man pitched from a saddle.

His mouth was grim, his eyes intent, his actions as machine-like as if they were not dictated by a brain. Deliberately, as he squeezed the trigger, he counted under his breath. One, two, three. There had been fourteen men in the party that hung Boone Ralston. He did not know how many had fallen in the attack on the Diamond J, but he did know that many were still alive.

The gunfire closed in on the house as if Peters's men realized that he was the sole remaining defender, and he knew that it was time to go. He wished for a horse, but he saw no way to reach the corral. He turned, glancing up the winding trail.

Afoot he stood little chance of escape in that direction. In a matter of minutes Peters's men would discover that the house was unguarded and would ride around it and up the trail.

His questing eyes found the rock shelf perched like a bastion above him, and a moment later he was struggling up the crude steps to the safety of the level top. He turned there, having now a full view of the yard, and he smiled a little as he squatted down, waiting for the searchers to round the house.

They came uncertainly, not sure that the defenders were indeed gone. He shot two of them, coolly, almost pleasurably, before the bullets from their companions drove him back from his roost to the brush behind.

He climbed, dragging himself up the nearly perpendicular rock face, grasping the twisted trunks and roots of the trees which grew tortuously out of the crevices. Below him, bullets lashed the brush where he had been.

Exhausted, he gained the top and dropped panting on a sharp hogback which ran at right angles to the canyon. He did not know how long he lay there. He had been a long time without sleep, and the blow on his head plus the exertion of the last few hours had sapped his great strength.

When he at last struggled to his feet the canyon below had sunk into grey darkness, lighted now only by the embers of the main house, which had burned nearly to the ground.

He stood sucking the cold air of early morning into his sore lungs, shivering under the creeping chill that had seeped clear to the marrow of his big bones.

He started along the ridge, trying to parallel the trail snaking up the canyon bottom. He needed food and he needed a horse, and the only place he could procure either would be at Crawford's.

He had no real idea how far off the outlaw town was, but he judged from the few references he had heard that it could not be too far — perhaps ten miles, or fifteen.

The ridge was gouged by side canyons where water had eaten its way down toward the trail, by rock upthrusts, some as big as a three story building. He circled them laboriously, panting in the thin mountain air.

The sun came up and climbed steadily into the center of the sky. Its rays were hot, and he removed his coat and doggedly went on.

In the afternoon he reached a cut so deep that it barred his passage. He sighed, looking down its abrupt slope and up the opposing side. Then tiredly he turned, circling back until he could find a route down to the canyon trail.

When he reached it he studied it carefully. Fresh hoof marks showed plainly in its traveled surface. A number of horses had passed this way during the night or the early morning hours.

They were too numerous to be only the survivors of the Diamond J crew, and he guessed that most of them had been made by Peters's men as they followed the fugitives. There were no tracks coming down which had been made since the last rain.

The certainty that the Colonel and his hirelings were in the mountains ahead of him sharpened his attention, and he went forward more warily, studying each short length of trail as he rounded one bend and then the next, careful not to be surprised.

It was deep dusk when he mounted a section of rising grade steeper than the rest, circled a rock shoulder which jutted out to turn the trail in a horseshoe, and saw before him a round valley perhaps half a mile across. The valley seemed to be completely encircled by the mountain fence whose higher peaks climbed until snow glistened on their crests in the last rays of the disappearing sun.

At Sanderson's level it had turned cold as soon as the sun ceased to beat upon the trail, and he had long since shrugged back into the protection of his coat.

He stopped, watchful. The valley was well wooded, mostly pole pine except where the small creek wound across the bowl, its banks studded by aspen, the white trunks seen like slender ghosts through the dark evergreens.

The trail wound among these trees until, near the cleared center of the bowl, it widened into a rutted camp street. There were eight buildings on this street, one of frame much larger than its fellows. The others were of logs, not much better than cabins.

Sanderson guessed the large building to be Crawford's store. It was a good eighth of a mile away, but even in the dying light he could see horses tethered at the rail, and he judged that the Colonel's crew was still in town.

He moved out of the trail into the shelter of the timber, and worked his way carefully forward, keeping as silent as he could, praying that he would meet no dogs.

His wide circle brought him to the rear of the store building at full dark, and he stood within the line of trees, the odor of cooking coffee coming out to make him more ravenous than he already was.

Sound echoed crisply from the front of the store, the rasp of men's voices, the scuff of boots, and then the sounds of horses, and in a moment he watched the Colonel's men ride out.

He moved forward to the building's rear wall and edged along it to the corner. Lamplight spilling through the store's front windows made a patch of brightness on the street, showing him that the rack before the entrance was empty.

He stepped out then, walking to the street's edge. There he stood, listening to the receding sounds as the riders were swallowed by the trees and the canyon. Then he climbed the two steps, crossed the old gallery and went into the store.

There was a fat man behind the counter, almost hidden by piles of merchandise which cluttered the place. The room was dusty, and some of the stock looked as if it had been on the shelves for twenty years.

The fat man turned. Fear widened his bead-like eyes, and his voice shook a little as he asked, "What's the matter now?"

"Matter?" Sanderson said.

"What'd you come back for?"

Sanderson understood then. The storekeeper had mistaken him for one of the riders who had just left. He said, "I wasn't with them. Who were they, Peters's crew?"

The fat man still stared at him, suspicion glittering deep in the black eyes. "Who are you then?"

"A stranger. I was with the Diamond J for a while."

The fat man pulled a red handkerchief from his hip pocket and mopped his wet face. "Lucky for you the Colonel's men didn't find you. They been here all day, running down the boys in the brush. Two they killed. Ford Patton and another rider they strung up, and two they took with them down to Fairview. Going to try them, they said, along with the girls."

"Girls?" Sanderson said hoarsely. "What girls? What are they going to try them for?"

The fat man grunted. "Arson, they said. Rustling, making the Colonel sign a false deed to his cows."

"What girls?"

"Ellen Jenner and Mary Ralston."

"But she didn't have anything to do with it — Mary Ralston I mean."

The man shrugged. "They claim she did, and the two men they took along volunteered to swear that she hired them and gave the real orders. Even the Jenner girl turned against her — said she and her brother had cooked up the whole deal to get their ranch back."

Sanderson could hardly believe his ears. "What kind of a country is this? A girl's father is murdered. Her ranch is stolen. She tries to keep out of the fight and keep her brother clear, and in return she gets arrested and her brother gets hung. Where I come from women are honored and treated with respect."

"Not on the Massacre, friend." The fat man came around the end of the corner, stepping between a coil of rope and a dozen stacked buckets. "Not with the Colonel running things, damn him. Threatened to burn this store, he did. Said I'd been harboring outlaws and brush jumpers. Might as well have burned it. After today most of the boys will clear out of the country for good, and then what will I do for customers?"

Sanderson said, "Which two men did they take with them?"

The storekeeper spat on his own floor with a fine disregard for cleanliness. "Never saw either of them before. They weren't regular Diamond J riders or they'd have got hung like Ford Patton and Southworth. And they weren't any of the boys who hole up around here in the winter. I'd guess they were drifters, hired when the fight started."

"Hear their names?"

The man scratched the thin rim of hair around the small balding spot at the crown of his overlarge head.

"One of them was called Boston, I think, and the other Hayes or Haynes or something like that."

Sanderson swore under his breath. Al Craig had been quick to take advantage of anything to save his worthless life. If he could escape by swearing in court that

Mary Ralston had engineered the attack on the Peters ranch, he would not hesitate to do so.

"Look," he said, "can I get a horse and something to eat?"

The fat man's eyes became wary. "They took most of my horses. I need the ones I've got left."

Sanderson reached inside his shirt, undid the pouch of his money belt and drew out three double eagles. The fat man stared at the gold, wetting his lips. "It's enough for the horse, but you'll need a saddle and —"

"There's not a horse in the country worth sixty dollars and you know it." Sanderson lifted his gun from the holster. "Maybe you'd rather I used this."

The man said hastily, "That's not necessary, friend. Come to think of it, there's a saddle in the back room someone left. You can have it. The sixty will be fine for the horse, just fine. Take your pick of any in the corral."

Later as Sanderson wolfed bread and cold meat at the kitchen table, washing down the tasteless meal with huge swallows of bitter coffee, the fat man asked curiously, "What you meaning to do?"

"Go to Fairview. Talk some sense into

that fool sheriff's head. He can't hold Mary Ralston for something she didn't do. Why, she had no more to do with any of it than you did."

"I know it." The storekeeper nodded. "But you're overlooking one thing, my friend. The Colonel has to get rid of Mary Ralston. He has to blacken her name. I heard some of his men talking, how they had hung the Ralston boy. They didn't like it much, but no one stands against Dred Stover and the Colonel. They were saying a lot of the valley people are going to sympathize with the Ralstons unless it's proved in court that she stirred up this mess — that she ordered the Colonel's ranch burned and hired gunhands like Boston to kill him."

"But she didn't. Ellen Jenner is different. They can hang her for all of me."

"Nothing will happen to Ellen Jenner." The fat man smirked with his thick lips. "I've known her since she was a little kid. She's the kind that gets her wants one way or another. Why, do you know what she was doing before they left here? She was making up to the Colonel, that's what."

Sanderson almost strangled on a mouthful of coffee. "She was what?"

"Making up to the Colonel like only she

knows how to play to a man. She went on about how she had never realized how strong he still is, that a man half his age couldn't have stayed in the saddle for as many hours as he had and still be ready to start for Fairview tonight."

Sanderson gaped. "You mean the Colonel would be fool enough to fall for that after what she's done to him in the last few weeks?"

The storekeeper blew out his heavy cheeks. "Who knows what an old man is idiot enough to believe when he's being worked on by a pretty woman? Seems like when a man's years get short his desires sharpen up, even if they're only in his mind. Wouldn't surprise me none if Ellen Jenner married him before she was through. She tried to take the valley one way and missed. What's to stop her from trying to grab it another way?"

Sanderson shook his head dazedly. There was nothing he could not now believe of Ellen Jenner; not a single thing in the world. For a moment he felt almost sorry for the Colonel. Then his mind hardened. The man was a vicious murderer. Sanderson meant to see him die.

Fourteen

Full daylight was on him again by the time he reached the burned out yard of the Diamond J. Some of the massive house timbers still smoldered, but aside from the small curl of smoke and the restless ashes there was little to quicken the scene of desolation.

Yesterday this had been a busy ranch. Today it was nothing at all, and again Sanderson was struck forcibly by the willful destructiveness of man.

He stepped down, loosened the reins and lifted the saddle, letting the tired horse graze along the grass which fringed the hard raw center of the yard.

From the saddlebags he brought the cold meat, the sourdough bread and the handful of coffee he had carried from the store. In the wreckage of the cook house he salvaged a blackened pan. He scoured it with creek sand, built his small fire and set it to boil.

He ate slowly, knowing the weariness of

long continued fatigue. After he had eaten he stretched out on the unyielding ground, wrapped in his coat, and slept until the sun, noon high in a cloudless sky, wakened him with its heat.

He rose, rekindled the sticks and heated the coffee remaining in the blackened pan. Then he caught up the horse and threw on the saddle the fat man had so generously given him, and swung up.

His body ached from the stony ground, and he was still groggy from lack of proper rest as he set the horse into the main trail and headed for Fairview.

He judged that it must be about thirty miles through the pass to the county seat, and he did not press the animal. He wanted to save its strength, for he did not know what he might run into when he reached the town.

The canyon wind and the movement of the horse cleared his mind, and he tried to consider his course of action. A well of anger roiled through him, such anger as he could not remember ever having experienced before. For years he had schooled himself to look at his work objectively. To him the pursuit of criminals had been a necessary arm of law. As the country filled law must follow, and his part had been to police the range, endeavoring to avert exactly such a thing as had happened in this valley.

His pursuit of Craig had been orderly despite his personal involvement with the people the man had killed. Even in the long, chilling ride across the mountains he had managed to hold himself well in hand.

Now it was different. He would ride into Fairview and he would rescue Mary Ralston no matter what he had to do to accomplish this end. He knew a hunger for vengeance, an ache to even the score with the men who had hanged Boone Ralston.

His feeling for the boy had little to do with it. In his own way, Boone Ralston had been as much at fault as the men who had put a rope around his neck and strung him to the tree branch.

The effect on the girl was what mattered to Sanderson. He admitted this honestly, for in some inexplicable way this quiet girl whom he barely knew had become for him the most important person in the world.

The town came as a surprise. After Massacre he had expected little more than a few huddled buildings nestling in the pass. Instead, Fairview looked as if it might contain three to four thousand people, and that very fact encouraged him.

Certainly a town of this size would not accept the domination of one man or one group of men. Certainly here there should be citizens who would stand up for justice.

It was dark when he rode up to the livery. He stepped down stiffly and delivered his horse to the hostler. The barn attendant was little more than a boy, yellow haired, with narrow eyes and a drooping, weak mouth above a weaker chin. He accorded Sanderson neither curiosity nor interest, and his answers to Sanderson's careful questions were coolly vague.

Yes, Colonel Peters and his crew were in town. He supposed they were at the hotel or at the Elkhorn saloon. His attitude showed plainly that he did not much care.

Yeah, there had been trouble in the valley below and they'd brought in four prisoners. Yeah, the town was some excited by the idea of women prisoners. But the boy did not share in the excitement. His only interest was to return to the office and resume his enjoyment of the dog-eared dime novel he had been reading by the light of a smoky lantern when Sanderson interrupted him.

Sanderson went down the street. Now that he was here he still did not know how to proceed, but automatically his steps turned toward the sheriff's office. He expected to find a deputy in charge, but when he pushed open the heavy door he saw Gilpen himself seated behind the scarred rolltop desk.

The sheriff was in his shirt sleeves, busy with some kind of a report. He did not look up immediately, and when he did, disbelief washed across his gaunt, weathered face.

"You — here?" he said.

"That I am," Sanderson assured him. "I judge you didn't expect to see me again."

"I sure didn't. If I was in your shoes I'd be a hundred miles away from here by now."

Sanderson suspected that this was very true. The sheriff did not strike him as a man likely to stand up against seemingly impossible odds. Also, he realized that he was an unwelcome witness as far as Gilpen was concerned. No one else outside of Peters and his crew could know that the sheriff had been present at the hanging of Boone Ralston. This fact Sanderson meant to use if he could. It was a slim hold indeed, but it was the only one he had.

"What do you want?" Gilpen asked.

"Mary Ralston."

"Huh?" Obviously Sanderson's answer startled Gilpen almost as much as his unexpected arrival had. "It's true then?"

"What's true?"

The sheriff tried to cover his blunder. "What they're saying about Mary Ralston."

"You don't believe it then?"

They stared at each other and Sanderson knew that Gilpen hated him, for he represented the sheriff's conscience.

"I do now." The sheriff stood up. "It's obvious, isn't it? You were a hired gun, bought to fight Peters, and now you come looking for the Ralston girl. If she didn't hire you, why are you here?"

"Is that the only reason you can think of?" Sanderson let his lip curl with deliberate contempt.

"No." The word burst from Gilpen. "We've got two witnesses — drifters who swear she hired them."

"One is a murderer," Sanderson said. "I don't know what the other is but I'm certain he's a liar. Mary Ralston had no more to do with the attack on Peters's ranch than you did."

"The Colonel thinks she did."

"And since the Colonel does your thinking for you, you think so too, is that it?"

"Damn it, you've got no call to talk to

me this way. Who do you think you are? What gives you the right to judge anyone? Your hands aren't so clean."

For answer Sanderson unbuttoned his shirt and drew two folded papers from the long pouch of his money belt. He laid them on the desk before the sheriff.

Gilpen hesitated for a long moment, then picked them up and unfolded them gingerly. One was the Utah warrant for the arrest of Al Craig for murder. The other was Sanderson's commission from the Western Cattlemen's Association.

Gilpen looked up at last, his face oddly drawn. "Who's this Craig?" He tapped the warrant.

"One of the men you're holding. He calls himself Boston here."

"You're sure of that?"

"I followed him over the ridge. He killed my partner and the girl I was going to marry."

Gilpen slowly refolded the papers and extended them. "Then what were you doing at the Diamond J?"

"Craig was there. Once I'd found him I wasn't going to let him out of my sight until I had a chance to arrest him when his friends weren't around."

The sheriff sat studying the man before

him. "I'm surprised you didn't kill him while you had the chance."

Sanderson started to say that as a law officer Gilpen of all people should understand. Then he didn't. This sheriff lacked the integrity which sets the real law officer apart from his fellows. He was a time-server, nothing more, a petty politician without the strength or will to stand against the men who had put him in office.

Sanderson said, "I'm not interested in Craig at the moment. I'm interested in Mary Ralston. Where is she?"

For a moment he thought Gilpen would refuse to answer. Then the sheriff said, "At the hotel. There's only one cell here. I needed it for Craig and the other rider. Besides, it's not a fit place for women."

Sanderson started for the door.

"Wait a minute. Don't try to go up there. Don't try to get her away. I've got three of the Colonel's riders watching those girls with orders to shoot anyone who even looks like they want to climb to the second floor. No one talks to them until after the court hearing in the morning."

"Who's the judge?"

"His name is Thorne. Bryant Thorne."

"Peters's man?"

"If you mean did Peters support him for office, yes."

"Where do I find him?"

"He'll be playing poker at the rear table of the Elkhorn saloon. He always is at this time of night."

"Good. I'll talk to him."

The sheriff stood up. "I don't know why I should waste time warning you, but I don't want any more trouble. There's been too much already. Peters's men are at the saloon. They're all over town, and as soon as they hear of your being in Fairview they'll start hunting you."

"I think I can take care of myself."

Gilpen measured him. "No doubt you're fast with that gun. You'd have to be to hold your job. But you'll need to be tonight. Stover's one of the fastest men in the country."

"With a broken arm?"

"He's as good with one hand as with the other. And don't think that because the Colonel is old he can't handle himself. He can still hit a half dollar at twenty feet, and I wouldn't want to try to draw against him."

"Thanks."

The sheriff blinked at him. "What are you thanking me for?"

"You just did me a favor," Sanderson

said. "I've sworn to myself to kill the men who hung young Ralston. It worried me a little, having to gun down a defenseless old man and a gunslinger with a broken arm. You relieve my mind." He turned and went out into the night.

Fifteen

The Elkhorn saloon held nearly a hundred men, lined against the long bar and grouped around the four card tables beyond.

Sanderson came in unobtrusively, pausing just inside the door to let his cool eyes range carefully across the crowd. Peters was not in the room, nor was Dred Stover.

He breathed a little easier. He had no doubt that some Box P men were present, but the chance that any of them except the Colonel or Stover would pay much attention to him was small.

He moved in slowly, working his way into the press of watchers around the tables, trying to be as inconspicuous as possible. The very size of the throng itself offered protection, but he had little time to waste. He did not trust the sheriff. He was almost certain that Gilpen would get to Peters at once with the word that he, Sanderson, was in town.

He had small difficulty in spotting

Thorne. The judge sat at the rearmost table, his back against the wall. He was a small man, perhaps sixty, perhaps older, with a thin face further lengthened by a grey goatee. As Sanderson reached the table Thorne raked in a big pot and one of the men across the table shoved back his chair in disgust.

"That's enough for me, Judge. I'd rather face you in court any time than sit in with you at a poker table."

Thorne grinned. "Trouble is, Howard, you know more about law than you know about cards. That's the difference between a lawyer and a judge. A judge has to know about both."

"And women," the man called Howard said as he stood up. "You know about women too, Judge. If you don't, you're going to learn tomorrow."

The sharp edge on Howard's voice made Sanderson look at him a second time. Howard was big, about forty, with curly black hair and a long nose.

A laugh ran through the crowd and Thorne's face froze. "Never discuss a case before it comes to trial."

"Unless it's with the Colonel," someone in the background said.

Thorne swiveled. At the moment he reminded Sanderson of a lone, lank wolf cornered by a pack of dogs. He sat still, slim fingers riffling the cards, eyes raking his tormentors.

Sanderson got the idea that the judge had few friends in this room. Suddenly the small man pushed back his chair, its legs making a grating noise on the splintered floor.

"I've had enough," he said.

Sanderson turned and preceded him to the door. No one paid any attention to him. Every eye in the big room followed Judge Thorne as he made his way toward the entrance.

On the dark street Sanderson waited for the judge to appear. The batwing doors came violently open and the little man burst through. He stopped not four feet from Sanderson, pulled a cigar from his vest pocket, bit off the end viciously and spat the shred of tobacco into the gutter.

"The fools." A match flared and the judge held the tiny flame against the end of the cigar, puffing vigorously. Sanderson moved up behind him on silent feet.

"Talk to you a minute, Judge?"

Thorne dropped the match as if it had burned his fingers. He swung around, his tone savage. "Who in hell are you?"

"The name is Sanderson."

Thorne glared at him with unreasonable fury. Sanderson guessed that he was a man ridden by temper, and like so many small men tried to make up what he lacked in size by feistiness.

"And what do you want?"

"Is there someplace where we can talk?"

"And why should I talk to you?"

Sanderson sensed the preciousness of his time. At any moment someone might come from the saloon. At any moment the sheriff might get word to Stover or the Colonel, and the hunt for him would be on.

He lifted the gun from its holster and poked the heavy barrel into the little man's side. "This is one good reason."

Judge Thorne bristled at him like an angry bull pup. "Go ahead — shoot me and bring the town down around your ears."

Sanderson's lips quirked grimly. Nothing he could do to this little man would increase his danger in the least. "You must have some sense," he said, "or you wouldn't be a judge. Get the chip off your shoulder and tell me where we can talk."

Thorne stared at him for a moment longer; then, ignoring the gun, he started up the street. The motion caught Sanderson by surprise. Still carrying the gun loosely in his hand, he trailed the judge. Thorne led him to a two-storied wooden building whose stairway opened between two store fronts, and started up the stairs.

Sanderson followed. The stairs were dark and he had no way of knowing whether the little man would swing above him and aim a blow at his unprotected head. But they reached the top without incident, and Thorne paused to strike a match, find the door lock and fit a key into its orifice.

Sanderson waited in the doorway until the judge struck a second match, found a lamp and lighted it to expose a long, narrow office room cluttered with a case of books, a rolltop desk, an iron letter press on a bare table, and three chairs.

The little man took off his hat, went around and sat down at the desk, again staring up at his visitor belligerently.

"All right, talk."

"About Mary Ralston," Sanderson said.

The judge flushed. "You heard me say in the saloon that I wouldn't discuss the case. I saw you standing by the card table."

"I heard you, but this is different."

"How different?"

"Those men were ribbing you. I'm serious."

Judge Thorne thrust out his goatee belligerently. "And what's your interest in Mary Ralston? She your girl?"

Caught off guard, Sanderson colored beneath his heavy tan. "I've only seen her three or four times in my life," he said gruffly. "I'm interested in justice."

The little man snorted. "Justice, he says. A blind woman with a pair of loaded scales. Listen, my friend. I've been a lawyer for forty years, a judge for nearly twenty, and I've seen damn little justice done in my life. The strong rule, the weak get shoved around. How much chance do you think your Mary Ralston will have in court even if she is innocent?"

"She is innocent. This is a frame-up."

Thorne's snort was louder than before. "It's always a frame-up when someone you like is being hurt. She'll have her trial tomorrow. That's the least I can do for her, not keep her sitting around waiting for what you call justice. But just remember this — I'm the judge, not the jury. I don't decide who is innocent or guilty. I merely sentence them when it's over. Now, get out of here and let me drink myself asleep."

"Just a minute. There's no evidence against her aside from the word of a murderer and a brush rider."

The judge squinted at him and said drily, "The Colonel swore out the warrant. He's got the Jenner woman as a witness too."

Sanderson started to say, "Oh, her," then held his words. Instead he unbuttoned his shirt, produced his warrant for Al Craig and his commission from the Cattlemen's Association.

The judge studied them much as the sheriff had, then shoved them back. "A Utah warrant."

"I want a Colorado one, holding Craig until I can get extradition papers from Denver. I don't want the sheriff turning him loose after this trial is finished."

The judge chewed his mustache, then shrugged and drew the forms from his desk.

When the warrant was filled out Sanderson pocketed it. "Now," he said. "I want to swear out warrants for Colonel Peters and Dred Stover."

Thorne's head snapped back. "You're crazy. Warrants for what?"

"For the murder of Boone Ralston."

They looked at each other a long while. Finally Thorne said, "In your business, if you are an Association detective, you know what false arrest means."

"I know."

"The Colonel will roast you alive. He'll have your job. You don't know how much weight he pulls, even with the Association."

"I can guess," Sanderson said.

"You'd better forget it."

"Meaning you're afraid to issue the warrants?"

For once, the judge took it calmly.

"Everyone has always said that I was nothing but an errand boy for the Colonel. I never bothered to argue. Those who said it are fools, and a man does not waste time arguing with fools. I've done my job, the way I saw it. I'll issue your warrants, but who in this town do you think will serve them? Not our friend the sheriff. Not in one million years."

"I'll serve them myself. I'm also a deputy United States marshal."

Thorne did not doubt his word. Many Association men were deputy marshals. But he said, "Mine isn't a Federal court and this is not a Federal matter."

"Maybe," Sanderson said. "But it's Federal land the Colonel is running cattle on. I'll take my chances. Just make out those warrants and I'll sign them."

The judge sighed. He made out the forms. As Sanderson added his signature there came the sudden pound of many feet on the stairs. The judge moved with surprising speed. He was out of his chair, across the room, locking the door.

Sanderson guessed that the sheriff had carried word to the Colonel, and this was the result.

Somebody tried the door, shaking the lock. Then Stover's heavy voice cut through the panel.

"Come on, Judge, open up. We know Sanderson's in there with you. We want him."

Sanderson had drawn his gun. The judge grabbed his arm and motioned toward the back window, pressing his lips close against Sanderson's ear.

"Out that way. Shed roof below."

Sanderson moved the length of the long room in a dozen quiet strides, slid up the sash and saw the slanted roof below. He stepped out onto it.

He half walked, half slid down its sloping angle until he reached the edge, and dropped lightly to the darkness of the alley.

Behind him he heard the rending, splintering crash as the lock broke free and the door slammed open, and above the turmoil the clear, sharp cry of the judge.

"You'll pay for that, Dred Stover. I'll have you in jail for breaking down that door."

Then Sanderson was running easily along the alley toward the cross street. He reached the corner, peered around it, saw no movement in the street and ducked across it to vanish into the mouth of the alley on the other side.

He hauled up then, breathing heavily, and moved forward at a more cautious pace. They were alerted now, and they would spread out, hunting the town for him. But in this kind of a hunt the quarry sometimes had an advantage. Everyone who moved before him was a potential enemy, while the searchers would have to be careful not to shoot each other.

Suddenly he came to the rear of the hotel. He stopped, gazing at the structure rising above him. There was no mistaking it. It was the only building with three stories in town. Somewhere in its upper regions, Mary Ralston and Ellen Jenner were being held under guard.

He stood studying the building for several minutes, trying to guess how the minds of the men hunting him would work. Would they expect him to try to escape the town, or would they guess that he might attempt to reach the girls?

The back part of the building, apparently housing the kitchen, was only a single story covered by a shed roof. From it wooden steps led upward to the top floors, providing some fire protection.

He found a rubbish can on which he could stand, reached the eaves of the kitchen roof and lifted himself over its edge to the rising surface above. He stayed there for a moment's rest, on his hands and knees, listening for sounds within the building.

As he waited there he heard voices at the alley mouth. Two men ran along it cautiously, their guns glinting faintly in the slim light.

He flattened himself on the roof, reaching down to free his gun and hold it in readiness. They paused opposite the door of the hotel kitchen.

"He wouldn't come down here," one of them said. "My bet is, he headed out of town as fast as he could move."

The other grunted. "You heard what Stover said. He may try to see the Ralston girl. We're supposed to tell the guards."

They opened the door below Sanderson and vanished into the building. Sanderson crept across the roof on his hands and knees to the fire escape, and began to climb it.

At the second floor level there was a

small platform. From this he peered through the window, along the carpeted hall lighted by two lamps in wall brackets. He was in time to see the two men from the alley mount the inner staircase and pause at the top.

A man, his chair tilted against the wall halfway between the stairs and the window where Sanderson watched, straightened and came erect as the two appeared, his hand dropping to his holstered gun. Then he recognized them and relaxed.

The window was loosely fitted and their voices came clear and strong.

"Where's the Colonel?"

"In his room, upstairs. What's happened?"

"That Sanderson ranny is in town. The sheriff says he's a stock detective with the Cattlemen's Association. Stover has the town turned out hunting him, but he may try to reach the girl. Watch it."

"He won't get up here. There's two men in the lobby and one watching the kitchen door."

"He wasn't watching when we came in. He'd gone to the bar for a drink, but he won't do it again. I gave him hell. He's back in the alley now."

Sanderson turned and peered over the

rail of the small platform in time to see the flare of a match, to see the man's head outlined as the watcher lit a cigarette.

He was nicely boxed. He could only hope that the guard in the alley would not look up. Apparently he didn't, for a moment later he disappeared under the roof overhang and Sanderson guessed that he had sat down, leaning against the kitchen wall.

He turned again to the window and saw the two messengers go back downstairs. The guard returned to his seat, propping his chair back against the wall, hooking his bootheels over the lower rung.

Holding his gun in one hand, Sanderson used the other to test the window. It was locked. He hesitated for a minute, looking upward at the platform on the third floor level; then he moved quietly up the steps, testing each weathered board before he trusted it with his weight.

As he reached the higher level he drew his breath in slow satisfaction. The window opening into the upper hall was half raised for air.

He peered in. As far as he could tell the hall was empty. One lamp burned in its wall bracket near the head of the stairway, but the rear of the corridor was in shadow.

Gently he slid the window up, the dry wood squeaking a little in its frame. He paused, waiting and listening, but apparently the sound had disturbed no one.

A moment later he was safe inside the hallway, his eyes ranging along the rows of closed doors which lined the passage on either side. Behind one door was the Colonel. The question was, which door?

He cat-footed forward, his boots making no noise on the worn carpet runner which covered the painted boards, pausing at one door and then another. No light showed under the first four at which he listened, but the half-inch crack beneath the fifth panel showed its ribbon of brilliance.

He stopped, smiling thinly at the line of light, and stood listening. He heard Ellen Jenner's voice first, a warm, lazy voice which even through the protection of the door made him cringe a little.

"All right. You whipped me, Colonel. You've whipped everyone you ever met. I can't understand why you never married, a man as attractive as you are."

"Never saw a woman I wanted."

"That's what I heard."

His laugh had the satisfied roundness of complacency. "Should say I never saw a woman I wanted bad enough to have around under foot all the time."

Her laugh matched his. "Men can change." She said it lightly, but underneath there was the core of hard purpose.

"Sure," he said. "You're licked. You know you're through in the valley unless you can marry me. I know your little tricks."

Her tone sharpened. "Very well. Let's play it off the top of the deck. But it isn't every man of seventy who has a chance at an unspoiled woman of twenty-five. I'd make you a good wife, Colonel, because it would pay me to. And the rest of your years would be a lot pleasanter for having me around. Good night."

The door knob turned. The door swung inward and Sanderson and Ellen Jenner faced each other.

Sixteen

"Sanderson!" She jumped backward into the room. Colonel Peters was in his shirt sleeves, seated in a chair beside the window. His coat and gunbelt lay upon the white cover of the bed. He moved with youthful speed, his reactions sharp and automatic, but he took only two steps before Sanderson brushed the girl aside and grabbed his arm.

"Don't try it."

Hate burned in Peters's black eyes. "I should have hung you along with young Ralston."

"You should have."

"I don't know how you got in here, but you won't find it as easy to get out. My men are all around this hotel. You're a fool. A man with any sense would be a long way from here by now. What do you hope to gain by coming here?"

For answer Sanderson pulled from his pocket the warrant he had sworn out against Peters and held it forward.

"You're under arrest."

"Arrest?" Peters's mouth sagged open. "Arrest for what?"

"Read the warrant. For the murder of Boone Ralston."

Peters unfolded the paper quickly. He stared at it in disbelief. "Thorne must be out of his mind."

"He's a judge," Sanderson said. "There wasn't much he could do except issue the warrant when I swore it out. You aren't very well acquainted with the law, are you, Colonel? You haven't paid much attention to it through most of your life."

Peters snorted. He started to tear the paper in two contemptuously, but Sanderson caught both his wrists. For an instant they struggled in silence, and then the old man quit, allowing Sanderson to take the paper away from him and return it to his pocket.

"What good do you think all this is going to do you?" Peters said.

Sanderson said, "I swore to kill you and Stover when I saw Boone Ralston hanging from that tree. I'd still rather break your scrawny neck than anything I can think of. But I'm willing to make a deal because there's a girl downstairs who has had enough. Sometimes it's wiser to forget vengeance than to make innocent people suffer."

He paused for effect.

"Withdraw your charges against Mary Ralston," he said, "and I'll tear up the warrant. Let us ride out, and you people in the valley can kill your own skunks."

The Colonel laughed. "You're in a fine position to make threats. Hand over your gun and I'll promise that nothing will happen to you. The Ralston girl will have to take her chances."

Sanderson slapped him across the mouth with the back of his hand. He said savagely, "Some people don't understand anything but force. I could kill you now. I could get your guards as they tried to come upstairs. I could take Mary Ralston out of here over the dead bodies of your crew."

"Why don't you then?"

Why didn't he? Compassion for Peters and the other men who might die had nothing to do with it. They deserved killing. It wasn't even his deep respect for the processes of law. It was rather the certain knowledge that the girl would not go. Mary Ralston's own stern code would never let her run away, even from a charge as unjust as the one which had been brought against her in the local courts.

Somehow he had to force this man before him to clear her name. Suddenly he turned on Ellen Jenner.

"I've got a warrant for this old man's arrest for murder," he said. "Also for Stover's arrest. If I make them stick the Colonel will be through in the valley. I doubt that even he could make the charges against you hold."

He could see the machinery of her mind pick up speed as she considered this newest possibility.

"What do you want from me?" she asked.

"To stand up in court in the morning. To tell the judge and the jury the truth — that no matter what anyone says Mary Ralston had nothing to do with the burning of Peters's ranch, nothing to do with forcing him to sign over his cattle."

She smiled then, bold and mocking.

"You heard him, Colonel. What do you bid against him?"

Peters cursed her, but even in his anger there was an aura of admiration. "I won't bargain with you, girl. I'd made up my mind to marry you, but now I've changed it. You switch sides too often."

"I haven't switched sides." She looked at Sanderson with deliberation. "I don't believe you have a chance. I do believe that

I'm more likely to get what I want by staying with the Colonel. So now it's your move."

He said, "You don't leave me much choice. Come on, Colonel. We're going downstairs. You're going to tell the guard on the second floor to throw down his gun. We'll lock him in one of the rooms. Then we're going down to the lobby and disarm those there. After that I'll take you to the sheriff's office, and I don't think even he will have the courage to turn you loose — not with this warrant on the record."

"You'll never make it," the old man said.

"If I don't you won't live to know about it. Put on your coat." He tossed the gunbelt out of the way to the far side of the bed and flipped the coat to the Colonel. As he did so heavy feet came running up the stairs and along the hall.

Sanderson's voice cut across the room. "Don't open that door or the Colonel will get a bullet in his head."

There was a sudden halt, a whispered conference in the hall outside, and Stover called, "Colonel? Colonel?"

"Answer him." Sanderson's gun jerked toward Peters.

The old man said, "Yes, Stover."

"What do you want us to do, Colonel?"

Sanderson said, "Clear out of the hotel and take your men with you. I'm going to march out of here in five minutes, with the Colonel ahead of me. If there is any trouble he dies first. Then I'll see how many more of you I can take with me."

He was watching the Colonel and the door. For the instant he had forgotten Ellen Jenner. She had been standing to his right, a little behind him as he swung to face the door. She had moved quietly, reaching across the bed as he talked, pulling the gunbelt toward her, lifting the Colonel's heavy gun. The first warning he had was when she shoved the barrel into his side.

"Drop it," she said.

For the space of a second Sanderson stood frozen. Then he heard Peters laugh. His impulse was to squeeze his trigger, but he knew for sure that he would be killed. If he escaped the girl's bullet the men in the hall would undoubtedly finish him, and with him dead Mary Ralston would have no chance at all.

He let the gun slide from his fingers and heard it thump on the floor. The Colonel scooped it up.

"Get over against the wall."

Sanderson moved to obey.

"It's all right now, Stover. Come in."

The door came open and Dred Stover and two men stomped into the room. Stover said, "How'd you get him?" and the Colonel pointed to Ellen Jenner, still holding the gun.

Stover grinned. Then he crossed over, spun Sanderson around with his good arm and hit him in the face. "That's for breaking my arm, saddle bum."

Sanderson wiped the blood from his mouth with the back of a hand and Stover hit him again, knocking him against the wall with a force which shook the building. Sanderson's shoulders seemed to have springs, for he rebounded from the wall, driving one hand into Stover's stomach, the other into the man's grinning face. The foreman backed away and one of his men clipped a gun down along the side of Sanderson's head, dropping him to his knees.

The Colonel said, "Takes a bit of punishment, doesn't he? There's some things in his pocket, a couple of warrants. Get them."

One of the men grabbed Sanderson's arms as he struggled upward, while Stover went through his pockets, finding the warrants for himself and the Colonel.

"Try his money belt."

They stripped the belt from his waist and the Colonel opened it, spilling out first two hundred dollars in double eagles, then drawing forth the Utah warrant for Al Craig, Sanderson's commission from the Cattlemen's Association and finally the bronze deputy United States marshal's badge.

"My, my," Peters said. "We've got a very important man here, Dred, a very important man. We should treat him more gently."

"We'd have hung him with young Ralston if you'd listened to me."

The Colonel nodded. "That's right," he told the foreman. "I should always listen to you."

"Shall we take him out of town and hang him now?"

"Probably as good a plan as any. How many people know he's in town and who he is?"

The foreman shrugged. "They say he was in the Elkhorn, but he didn't speak to anyone, didn't even have a drink. Aside from the sheriff and the judge no one knows but the boys who have been hunting him."

"Good." The Colonel smiled at Sanderson as if he found the idea pleasing. "I don't suppose anyone will ever quite know what happened to you."

That, Sanderson thought as he wiped his bruised lips, was probably true. The Association would wonder when they failed to hear from him. The Utah authorities would wonder when their warrant for Craig was not returned, but they would not even know in which direction to look.

He thought of Mary Ralston and the realization that he would not see her again went through him like a knife. Why hadn't he killed Peters when he had the chance? Why hadn't he taken the girl out of this hotel by violence?

He heard the Colonel give the order, and the two men shoved him from the room. They herded him down the first flight, then the second, to the lobby below. Behind him, the old man swore sharply.

He turned his head. Peters was not looking at him, but at a small figure standing against the hotel desk, watching their descent.

The judge had his elbows hooked over the edge of the high desk as if it were a bar. His hat was shoved back and his goatee seemed to stand straight out as he looked upward.

He appeared very small, and he was not wearing a gun.

Peters bulled past Sanderson and his two guards and walked over to confront the judge.

"What are you doing here, Thorne?"

A devil of mockery danced in the judge's eyes. "I might say I was just loafing, Colonel. I might even say it was none of your business, this being a public lobby even if your boys have been using the building for a jail."

"Come to the point."

Thorne indicated Sanderson with a slight sweep of his hand. "I had a talk with this young fellow earlier. I kind of liked the way he sized up. He believes in law. It might surprise you that I've got some of the same notions myself."

"I've got no time for foolishness, Thorne."

"No," Thorne said. He seemed to be speaking to himself. "You haven't any time for foolishness unless you start it yourself. What do you mean to do with him?"

Sanderson said through stiff lips, "There was some talk of hanging."

One of his guards grabbed him, twisting his arm. "Shut up."

"Hanging, is it?" The judge pushed his

hat a little farther back on his head. "And what's the charge?"

"This isn't your courtroom." The Colonel sounded about ready to explode.

"No." The judge looked around in pretended surprise. "It isn't any courtroom, is it? Just when was this man convicted, and of what?"

"He helped burn my ranch."

"That's a serious charge. Others are being held on a like indictment. I'll expect to see him in court in the morning."

The Colonel said tensely, "Get out of here. Walk out and I'll forget what you've said."

The judge didn't appear to hear him. "And he's a detective for the Cattlemen's Association, and a deputy U.S. marshal. Questions will be asked if he should disappear without a trace, questions asked by men outside this valley, men who never heard of you, Colonel, and who would not be impressed if they had."

"Are you threatening me?" The Colonel took a step toward him, palming his gun butt. "For one cent I'd blow your silly head right off your shoulders."

The judge smiled puckishly. "That I wouldn't advise. I'm a character in this town. For years I've played a conscious part until I'm as much a part of the town as is the courthouse. I'm the law as far as Fairview's citizens are concerned. They laugh at me, but they laugh at me because they like me."

Peters was baffled. He could not have been more surprised if one of his steers had suddenly turned on him and refused to be driven to market.

"What do you want me to do?" he said. "Let this man go free? Let him shoot up the town, and block the trial?"

"Put him in jail. That's what we have jails for. Bring your charges in court tomorrow. I hardly think you'd find a jury in the whole country who would go contrary to your wishes, so long as you follow the letter of the law."

Peters made his decision. He even managed to sound a little sheepish as he said, "I guess you're right. Okay boys, march him down and tell Gilpen to lock him up."

Surprisingly the small judge winked at Sanderson above the Colonel's head. Sanderson did not understand exactly what the wink was supposed to convey, but it encouraged him.

"They took my papers, Judge. Will you get them back for me?"

Thorne seemed to consider with judicial

gravity. "Seems a fair request. You want to give them to me, Colonel?"

Peters hesitated. "Shouldn't they be turned over to the sheriff for safekeeping, now that we're following the rules?"

"I'll do that. I'll come along down to the jail."

Still reluctant, Peters passed them over. "I guess you don't need these warrants against Stover and me?"

"I'll take those too. They've been issued. There's a record."

He stuffed them into his pocket along with the warrant for Craig and Sanderson's commission and badge.

The sheriff was alone in his office. It was almost as if he had purposely remained indoors, out of the way until after Sanderson was disposed of.

He blinked at the prisoner and the men with him, slowly accepted the papers the judge handed to him, and put them in the top desk drawer.

The Colonel said a little pompously, "I'm charging this man with leading the Diamond J riders in the attack on my ranch, with burning it and with forcing me to sign a Bill of Sale for my cattle. I say that he was hired by Mary Ralston for that purpose, that he took over the Diamond J crew and despite Ellen Jenner's efforts to stop him, led them against me."

Sanderson slumped wearily. So Ellen Jenner had won her point. The Colonel was busy whitewashing her, throwing the blame onto him and Mary Ralston.

The sheriff glanced at him. "You want to say anything?"

"I'll save it for the courtroom."

"Come on then." The sheriff got a ring of keys. He opened the door at the rear of the office and led the way along a short hall to the door of the single cell. Al Craig had been standing, gazing out of the only window. The man called Haynes sat on one of the two strap bunks.

Craig swung around as the door opened and gaped at Sanderson. "So they caught you too." His shoulder was still bandaged where Sanderson's bullet had clipped him, but the wound could not have been deep for he used the arm with no apparent difficulty.

The sheriff relocked the door after his latest prisoner and said with a sour grin, "Sorry if you're crowded. You can take turns sleeping." He went down the hall and closed the office door behind him with a bang.

Sanderson moved over and sat down beside Haynes, who made room for him grudgingly. Craig was examining him with lively curiosity.

"Where'd they catch you?"

"What difference does it make? What's this talk that you're turning state's evidence — putting the whole blame on the Ralston girl?"

"Well, her brother hired me in the first place, and he said it was her idea, and —"

"You're lying." Sanderson said it pleasantly, but there was a gritty sound to his voice. "You know the Jenner woman started this whole thing and that Mary Ralston had nothing whatever to do with it."

Craig swung again to the window as if the argument had small interest for him. "We're wasting our breath. We're both caught, and we both want to get out of here. Right?"

"I suppose so."

"So if you're smart you'll play it the way Haynes and I are playing it. We're saying what the Colonel wants said. Even the Jenner girl is that smart. She's going along."

Sanderson stood up. "What I don't get is why Peters is so all fired anxious to hang all this on Mary Ralston. What does it buy him?"

Craig grinned. Then he started to laugh. "That's simple," he said. "Ellen Jenner told us on the ride in. Seems last year the old goat got ideas where the Ralston girl was concerned. He went to her restaurant and he made his pitch. She ordered him out of the place but he didn't go. Instead he followed her back into the kitchen and she tossed a skillet full of hot grease all over him. He swore then he'd get her, and I guess he's got her now."

He broke off, for the office door had come open at the end of the cell hallway and the sheriff appeared.

"Hey, Boston. Come over to the bars."

The man moved slowly across the cell, a little swagger in his walk as if he knew that he had made his deal with the Colonel and that this sheriff could do nothing to hurt him.

"What do you want?"

"Your name Boston, or is it Craig?"

All of a sudden the swagger was gone. Craig's body stiffened. He stood like carved stone, and the voice deep in his throat was a croak.

"What are you talking about?"

"There's a warrant in my desk for you. A warrant from Utah. He had it." The sheriff pointed toward the seated Sanderson. "He claims you're the man he's after. Says he trailed you over the mountains, that you're a murderer. He claims to be a stock detective for the Cattlemen's Association."

Craig stood now, grasping the bars as if he would pull them apart. The sheriff grinned at him, turned and walked back along the hall.

Sanderson was aware that the man on the bunk beside him had drawn away. A stock detective. It was one of the worst things an outlaw like Haynes could think of, far worse than a sheriff or a U.S. marshal. Stock detectives were noted for never giving up the hunt, never stopping once they had ridden on a rustler's trail.

Craig turned, and Sanderson read the burning hate in the man's eyes. Craig had more cause to fear him than did Haynes, for Craig had murder hanging over his head. Worse, the murder of a woman.

For an instant Sanderson puzzled over the sheriff's action; then he understood with quick clarity. This was not the sheriff's idea, but the Colonel's. The Colonel no longer dared to hang him, not with the judge around to tell what happened to anyone who made inquiry. But the Colonel had planned his death as certainly as if he had placed a noose around Sanderson's neck with his two hands.

These two men would kill him.

He could see the sheriff's pretended surprise when his battered body was found in the cell. He could hear the Colonel saying to the judge:

"How did we know they would find out he was a stock detective, that they would beat him to death?"

The judge might not believe it, but what could Thorne do? And when his employers got around to making a search they would be told only that unfortunately he had met death at the hands of a couple of killers with whom he had shared a cell.

Craig was leaning back against the bars, flexing the hand of his wounded arm as if reassuring himself that he could use the fingers properly.

"So I was right," he said. "You did follow me. I should have killed you then. There was something about you didn't smell right from the first. I can usually spot a John Law as far as I can see one."

Sanderson let his hands slip off his legs to rest on the thin blanket over the straw mattress. He curled his fingers around its edge to give him leverage when the time came to spring.

There was very little room. The cell, he judged, was about five by seven, and the two bunks hanging from the wall occupied a good third of the space. It would be brutal, close in fighting, two of them against him. Even handicapped as Craig was by the wounded arm, they certainly held the advantage.

And there would be no holds barred. They were out to kill him. Nothing else would satisfy. To them he was a Judas, a spy who had wormed his way into the Diamond J crew, and they dreaded nothing in the world more than an undercover agent, a spy.

All the hate and fear they had ever felt for the forces of the law would be directed against him.

As if by some prearranged signal Craig jumped, and at the same time Haynes shot out an arm, intending to lock it around Sanderson's throat from behind.

But Sanderson caught the movement from the corner of his eye. He used his powerful arms as springs to lift himself off the bunk and propel his hard body across and against the opposite wall, swinging as he reached it, jarring his shoulder with the force of his impact against the heavy planks.

He whirled to face them.

Al Craig had been unable to check his driving rush. Momentum carried him half across the bunk and his chin hit Haynes's shoulder with a shock which knocked Haynes backward across the thin mattress.

Sanderson might have rushed in then, but he chose to wait. If he dived forward they would be tangled together in one struggling heap, and since there were two of them they would have the best of it.

Had there been more room to maneuver he would have had a certain confidence of handling them both, but in this limited space he feared that they would get him down. If one managed to hold him the other could beat him into insensibility.

He stood beside the wall watching them untangle, watching first Craig and then Haynes struggle to his feet. Both were wary now.

"Look," Craig said, wiping his mouth with the back of his good fist, "we rush him. Grab his arms. You can hold him better than I can. You hold him, I'll finish him."

"Always looking for someone to do your work," Sanderson jeered. "Pity you couldn't have found someone to do it the night you skulked around outside the hotel in Steadman and shot Martha Horn and Will Austin."

Craig swore at him and charged. As he did so Sanderson crossed his right to the jaw and drove his left into the man's stomach, knocking him backward to the bunk. Then he sidestepped so that Haynes's grabbing hands caught only a partial hold on his shoulders.

The man tried to drag him forward. Sanderson surprised him by coming willingly, breaking the grip as he came in, lifting his knee to drive it sharply into Haynes's groin.

The man doubled over with pain. Sanderson straightened him with a short uppercut full on the chin, and then as he fell back toward the bunk, drove a heavy left into the short ribs which made him grunt.

Haynes fell, striking the edge of the bunk with the small of his back and lying half on, half off the lumpy surface.

At that moment Craig jumped on Sanderson's back, wrapping his good arm around his neck, his legs around Sanderson's belly, and took him to the dirty floor, yelling to Haynes for help as they went down.

The man rolled off the bed, groggy. His hands sought and found Sanderson's hair and he pounded his head against the floor.

Sanderson tried to roll free. He only succeeded in rolling them all under the edge of the bunk, but at least he managed to break the scissors hold of Craig's legs and to draw up his knees between them, using them as a lever to force the man away from him, feeling the choking arm slip along his throat until Craig rolled off. Then he reached up, got hold of the center finger of Haynes's right hand and bent it backward until the bone snapped.

The man's high, wild cry filled the cell and the grip on Sanderson's hair was gone. He rolled out from under the bunk and got a sharp kick in the side of the head from Craig's boot, and felt his senses swim as he came up to his knees and then to his feet. He was having trouble breathing, and brushed his hand across his nose and saw the streak of crimson which his blood left.

Craig was charging again. The sharp clarity with which Sanderson had entered the fight was gone. He felt as if he had been drugged, as if he were seeing through a fog, hearing through a blanket. Pain was a dull thing now, remote, removed as if it were happening to someone else and he sensed it only indirectly.

He knew that he hit Craig once, twice,

three times, and that the man backed away. He knew that Haynes charged him from behind and that one of the man's blows sent him sprawling on the bunk, striking his head against its sharp edge.

He knew that they both grabbed him, that Craig hauled him upright, that Craig's arm was again around his neck, dragging him backward, and that Haynes was battering at his face.

He kicked out with both feet, his whole weight on Craig, and felt both boots land solidly in Haynes's stomach Craig was jolted back, his grip broken, and Sanderson fell to the floor on top of him. He reached over his head, got a handful of Craig's hair and dragged the struggling man over his shoulder.

He knew vaguely that he was beating Craig's head against the bunk support, and that the man had ceased to struggle. But he kept on, lifting the senseless head by the hair, dropping it to the edge of the bunk, lifting, dropping, lifting, dropping, as mechanical as raising and lowering the handle of a pump.

He did not know whether it was his personal hatred for the man, his grief at the deaths of Martha Horn and Will Austin, or merely the subconscious knowledge that unless he stopped Craig the man would kill him.

What halted him finally he did not know. Perhaps sheer physical exhaustion. He did not actually know whether Craig was alive or dead. He did not care. He let go his grip on the bloody hair and the man slumped to the floor, his battered head a mass of reddish welts.

Over in the corner, Haynes lay in a heap. His head had struck the wall when Sanderson kicked him in the stomach.

Whether Sanderson passed out or whether he merely slept he could not tell. He roused finally to hear the click of the cell door, to hear the sheriff say, "My God," in a startled voice as he came into the cell.

Then, suddenly, he was alert, his mind grasping the full situation, and he stopped the groan which had almost issued from his lips.

Gilpen was careless. Obviously he thought all three were unconscious, all perhaps dead. He bent over and pulled Sanderson's body off of Craig, hauling him into the corner, then knelt and felt for Craig's heart action.

His back was toward Sanderson, his head bent forward, the handle of his holstered gun a tempting target only inches from Sanderson's hand. Sanderson lay there watching it for what seemed hours, weighing his chances.

If the sheriff heard him move, if Gilpen even sensed what he was about before he had the gun, everything was lost. In his present battered condition he would stand small chance against Gilpen's strength. Cautiously he drew his knees up under him. The gun's grip was still tantalizingly close, but he could not reach it, not lying flat on the floor.

He made his knees. He reached out then, trying to steady the shakiness of his arm. His fingers closed about the smooth, worn wooden plates and he jerked the heavy weapon from its resting place, feeling a new sure strength run through him when he had it safely in his grasp.

The sheriff felt the motion and started to jerk around.

"Hold it," Sanderson said. "After what you did to me I should blow you in two."

Gilpen stayed on his knees. Sanderson dragged himself up with the help of one hand against the wall. He stood there, getting the feel of his legs under him, taking his time about it. Gilpen might have another gun, a holdout concealed somewhere about his person, but he doubted it.

"Crawl over to the other wall," Sanderson said.

Gilpen crawled. Sanderson stepped back through the partly open cell door. The key still hung in the lock, the big ring with the other keys dangling from it.

Sanderson slammed the door and pulled out the key. Gilpen had risen to his feet.

"Hey, you can't leave me in here with them," he said in a scared voice. "They may be dead."

"If they are they won't hurt you," Sanderson told him. "It isn't your fault that I'm not dead, so from here on out don't ever get in my way." He turned and went along the hall, opening the door to the sheriff's office cautiously to make sure the room beyond was empty. Then he crossed to the desk, tossed the key ring on the top, pulled open the top drawer, found his warrants and his badge and stuffed them into his pocket.

There was a pump and a watering trough at the side of the building. At the trough he washed his hands and face free of the caked blood. The cold water stung, and the cold wind from the hills made him shiver. The street was deserted. The town of Fairview still slept.

He moved along the street cautiously, his

hand on his gun. Now that he was free he had no intention of being taken again. At the livery he found the hostler asleep, wrapped in a blanket on a pile of hay in the end box stall. He looked down at the man in the light from the lantern he had taken from the smelly office. His every inclination was to find another blanket, to stretch out in the barn too, and give his aching muscles rest.

But the sheriff's cries from the jail window might wake someone in the town and start the hunt all over again. He had to go on.

He found and saddled his horse, and with the hostler still sleeping, extinguished the lantern and rode out of the barn.

A side draw led off the trail about three miles from town. He turned into it, rode for perhaps a quarter of a mile, dismounted, unsaddled and picketed his horse. Then, wrapped in the saddle blanket, his head cushioned on the saddle, he went to sleep. He slept with the gun clasped tightly in his right hand.

Seventeen

The old courtroom at Fairview had seats for sixty people, and every one of them was filled when Judge Bryant Thorne appeared and his clerk called the court to order.

The sheriff appeared, looking shaken and unkempt after his experience of the night before. Then four deputies sworn in as specials for the occasion — all members of the Box P crew — herded in the prisoners and the witnesses.

Haynes needed help to walk. Craig looked as if his head had been run through a meat grinder. Ellen Jenner was surprisingly fresh and youthful in a long dress of summer print, and the hat she wore brought whispers from half the people who filled the courtroom.

Mary Ralston was the last to enter, save for the deputy who escorted her. She still wore the riding clothes in which she had been taken, a divided skirt and a waist made from a man's shirt.

Her head was bare and the delicately

wrought mask of her face concealed her true feelings. She and Ellen Jenner were the only women in the court. Women as a general thing did not appear at such gatherings. She walked with steady step to the counsel table where the young lawyer who had been appointed to defend her sat fiddling nervously with the three books he had carried from his meager office, hoping that by so doing he might impress the jury.

The lawyer had no illusions. He had only been practicing a year, but in that time he had learned that the only real law in this whole county was administered by Colonel Peters in any way he saw fit.

The lawyer's name was Rudd. He had come from Ohio because of health, and had not yet adjusted himself to this high country and its ways. He glanced sidewise at his client as she took her seat in the chair at his side, and was struck by her beauty, by her poise, by her refusal to display emotion.

It seemed incredible to him that anyone would attack her. He had heard the story about the Colonel's attempted attentions, about the skillet of hot grease. The story was all over town, and it seemed to him that every man in Fairview should have been willing to rise to her defense.

But these men in the serried rows of seats

behind him looked almost indifferent. It was hard to accept that they had so lost their individuality that they would sit quietly by and see this girl railroaded to the new prison at Canon City merely because of their fear of Peters. Yet his year had taught him that dominance is by habit, and these people had long since acquired the habit of obeying when the owner of the Box P spoke.

The knowledge galled him, filling him with frustration, making him realize how utterly powerless he was to help his client.

Whatever he said, whatever evidence he produced, the verdict was already written in the minds of the men who sat sweating in this room.

It was hot. The big windows in the thick courtroom walls were raised and those who had not been able to find other seats squatted in the wide sills.

Rudd did not challenge as the jury was chosen. Why challenge? Why do anything? His own sense of dignity counseled that he rise to his feet and request that the judge allow him to withdraw from the case, but such action would be a slap in the face of the girl beside him. She had no other friend in the world, unless you could count the man named Sanderson.

He glanced at the sheriff. The story of

how Gilpen had locked Sanderson in the cell with the two men, of the resulting fight and of how the sheriff had wound up in his own jail, a prisoner, was also all over town. In a community like Fairview few secrets could be kept.

And Sanderson was gone. Sanderson's horse was missing from the livery stable although the hostler had sworn that he had heard nothing during the night. The chances were that Sanderson would never be heard of around here again.

Craig and Haynes were led before the judge. Both pleaded guilty to taking part in the attack on the Peters ranch.

Rudd's face tightened as he listened. He knew what the prosecutor and the Colonel were up to. These men would throw themselves on the mercy of the court. Then they would be called upon to testify that they had been hired by the quiet girl he was asked to defend.

The judge glared down at the two men as he accepted their guilty pleas. "You will be returned to this court tomorrow morning for sentencing." His eyes took in the marks on Al Craig's head and face, the battered condition of Haynes, but he offered no comment.

"Next case."

The spectators stirred expectantly as Ellen Jenner was called. She moved forward gracefully, sure of herself as if she had not a worry in the world. "Ellen Jenner, you are charged with arson, the willful destruction of property at the Box P ranch. How do you plead?"

"Not guilty."

The prosecutor was on his feet. "Your Honor."

The judge looked at him over the square steel rimmed glasses he had perched near the end of his nose.

"Yes, Mr. Attorney?"

"It has come to our attention that the prisoner, while present during the attack on the Box P, acted under duress. She has made a voluntary statement." He brought the paper forward to lay it on the judge's desk. "Because of this, and her expressed willingness to turn state's witness, I request that the indictment against her be withdrawn."

Thorne fiddled with the papers on his desk. "This is highly irregular."

"Yes, Your Honor."

"Under the circumstances I'll continue her hearing until tomorrow. Next case."

"Mary Ralston."

Everyone in the courtroom leaned forward. She turned to look at her lawyer, who nodded slightly. She rose and walked to the judge's desk.

He peered down at her, no softening on his small face, consulting the papers before him.

"Mary Ralston, you are charged with arson in connection with the burning of the Box P. You are charged with inciting a riot and with hiring gunmen with the purpose of attempted murder. How do you plead?"

"Not guilty."

He peered at her again, as if he thought that he could break down the mask of her face with his stare. "Are you represented by counsel?"

She turned a little as Rudd moved forward to her side. "Yes, Your Honor."

Thorne shuffled his papers. To those who knew him it was plain that he did not like any part of the proceedings, and did not quite know how to stop them.

"Are you ready to proceed?" He addressed Rudd.

"Yes, Your Honor."

"Is the state ready?"

The prosecutor stood up. "Yes, Your Honor."

"All right, summon the jury."

They filed into the box.

Rudd looked them over. He wished he had challenged some of them. But on second thought, what difference would it have made?

The state's attorney posted himself before the jury box. His voice was low, musical, confidential. He said:

"The state will prove that Mary Ralston, in association with her brother, did conspire to drive Colonel Peters from the Valley of the Massacre; that through her brother she employed some seventeen gunmen with the understanding that they would resort to any necessary tactics to achieve that end, even to murdering the Colonel.

"We will show that these men were told by both Boone Ralston and his sister that Miss Ellen Jenner of the Diamond J was a party to the plan and that the Diamond J was to be used as headquarters for the operation, but that when they arrived at the Diamond J they learned that in reality she was little more than a prisoner, and that she did everything in her power to prevent the tragic events which followed."

He stopped. He walked solemnly back to the desk.

The judge sounded bored. "Call your first witness."

"Miss Ellen Jenner."

She stepped up gracefully to take the stand. In a controlled, throaty voice she spun her story. Listening to her, the defense lawyer knew she was lying, but there was nothing he could put his finger on, nothing he could question.

She told it convincingly — how her father out of all the ranchers in the valley had always managed to stay out of trouble with the Colonel, how surprised she was when the gunhands rode up to the Diamond J and said they had been employed by Boone Ralston and his sister. She related how she had tried to confront Boone and the girl only to be told that she had no choice; that she either went along with their plans and shared the valley with them after Peters's death or her ranch would be destroyed by their hired gun crew.

"And by whom were these men led?"

The question was asked casually, as if the prosecuting attorney did not really care.

The girl on the stand took her time answering. Then she said distinctly, "A man named Sanderson. A hired gunfighter if I ever saw one."

"Thank you." The prosecutor sounded very pleased. He made a little bow to Rudd.

"Your witness."

"No questions," Rudd droned.

From the corner of his eye Rudd saw Mary Ralston turn to him and saw the shadow in her dark eyes, as if she knew that he too had sold her out. But there was not a thing he could do. Ellen Jenner had herself under full control. She was an accomplished liar, and anything he could ask her would only further cement in the jury's mind the conviction that she was telling the truth.

He watched as first Craig and then Haynes took the stand. Their stories were nearly identical, suggesting that they had been rehearsed. Both admitted being drifters. Both said that they had ridden into the valley by chance, that they had been approached by Boone Ralston and taken by him to his sister's restaurant, where they were offered five hundred dollars apiece if they would sign on for the war with Peters.

The prosecutor asked the same question of each. "Then who do you think was the instigator of this attack?" And both had answered looking straight at the girl they accused:

"Mary Ralston."

In neither case did Rudd cross-examine.

The men were lying. He was sure of it. Oh, they had probably been recruited by young Ralston. All the evidence seemed to point to the fact that Mary's brother had been deeply involved in this plot. But did it implicate the girl, his client?

Theoretically the burden of proof was on the prosecution, but he realized with sickening certainty that in this case the positions had been reversed.

He rose. His opening speech to the jury was a plea, for fairness, a recital of the wrongs the girl and her brother had suffered at the Colonel's hands.

Then he put her on the stand. "Did you at any time, in any way, take part in a plan to drive the Colonel from the valley?"

She looked levelly at Peters. He was sitting in the aisle seat of the second row behind the counsels' tables.

"I did not," she said.

"Did you know that your brother was plotting such a course with Ellen Jenner?"

"I suspected it."

"What did you do?"

She controlled her voice now with visible effort. "I tried to talk to him. I tried to warn him that no good would come of it, that no one in the valley had ever fought Peters and gained by it."

"Then you never hired a gunman to join in the fight? You've heard the testimony of these two men."

She said slowly, distinctly, "They are lying."

A rustle ran through the crowd.

"That's all," Rudd said. "Your witness, sir."

The prosecutor waved his hand. "No cross-examination."

"The witness may stand down."

Mary Ralston stepped out of the box.

"Your next witness?" Judge Thorne said.

"I have no other witness, Your Honor."

"Just a minute."

Jim Sanderson's big frame filled one of the side windows. The courtroom spectators had been so intent on what the judge and the attorney for the defense had been doing that no one had seen Sanderson ride his horse along the side of the building, swing from the saddle to the sill and duck beneath the raised glass.

The guards whom Colonel Peters had placed before the building entrance had long since slipped inside to share the excitement, confident that the man they watched for was miles out of the country.

The sightseers parked on the edge of the window sill slid quickly out of the way, and

Sanderson dropped to the floor. His face bore the cuts and bruises of last night's battle, and his was the face of a man calmly, grimly, indomitably seeking another battle.

"I think you have another witness, sir." He addressed the defense attorney in a polite, tight-lipped monotone.

Rudd looked helplessly at his client. Mary Ralston was staring at Sanderson as if she had never seen him before.

"Do you know him?" he whispered.

She inclined her head, ever so slightly.

"What's his name?"

"Jim Sanderson."

So this was Sanderson.

Arnold Rudd might never become a great lawyer. He had admitted this to himself long ago, but he grasped an opportunity now as a drowning man clutches at anything within his reach.

He turned to the bench. "If it please Your Honor, I call James Sanderson to the stand."

Sanderson cut across to the aisle and followed it to the front of the courtroom. He stood toweringly erect in the witness box as the clerk administered the oath. His eyes met those of Colonel Peters and he smiled. The abrasions about his mouth drew the smile into an ominous grimace.

Rudd came forward. Never, he thought, had an attorney been so in the dark in trying to question a witness. All he knew about this man was that he had been arrested last night and locked in a cell with two of the other witnesses, who apparently had tried to kill him. Somehow he had trapped the sheriff, locked the officer in his own jail and escaped. No one in Fairview had expected ever to see him again, but here he was, somehow dominating the trial.

"Your name?" Rudd said hoarsely.

"James J. Sanderson."

"Your occupation?"

"I am a deputy federal marshal for the northern district of the state of Utah. I am also employed by the Western Cattlemen's Association as a stock detective."

A murmur of surprise rippled through the room, but no one in the hot crowd was more surprised than Rudd. He dredged his memory, trying to recall everything he had heard about this man during the morning. The town had been alive with gossip about the fight in the cell, about the prisoner's escape and the sheriff's imprisonment in his own jail.

"I see." Rudd used the meaningless words to cover his own confusion. "Are you in the valley on business?" He asked the question because he did not know what else to ask.

"Yes."

"What business, if I may ask?"

"I have a warrant for that man." The witness pointed to Al Craig, in the first row. "For murder."

Craig shifted uneasily, his battered face showing his uncertainty.

"A warrant? He killed someone in Utah?"

"Two people. One was a woman."

The buzz in the courtroom grew louder.

Rudd was completely at sea. He had no idea what to ask next. He groped helplessly, then fell back on a time-honored device.

"Will you tell us in your own words what has happened to you since you rode into the valley?"

"I object." The state attorney was on his feet. The judge peered at him.

"On what grounds?"

"What happened to the witness is not material to this case."

The judge seemed to consider. He looked at the defense attorney. "Are you developing background for the testimony?"

"Yes, Your Honor."

"The witness may proceed."

Sanderson had been on the stand many times before, and he knew the value of evidence almost as well as did the judge. In a low, intense voice he told everything that had happened to him since riding through the pass: of his first meeting with Boone Ralston, of Mary's request that he get her brother free of the valley, of joining the Diamond J crew for the purpose of staying close to Al Craig.

The state attorney fumed. Colonel Peters talked angrily to Stover in a low tone. Stover rose and made his way out of the court.

Rudd took up the questioning. "When you joined the Diamond J did you find that Mary Ralston was the real boss?"

"I did not."

"Who was?"

"Ellen Jenner."

Ellen Jenner sat rigidly, watching Sanderson.

"Now, did you at any time learn that Mary Ralston was in any way involved with the attack on Colonel Peters?"

"I did not. Ellen Jenner led the attack on the Box P herself. She forced him to sign a bill of sale for his cattle, then she ordered Al Craig and another rider to take Peters out and shoot him."

"Objection." The prosecutor was almost jumping up and down in frustration.

"Overruled." The judge sounded bored.

"What happened then?"

Sanderson went on, telling of his rescuing Peters and Stover, of riding back to Massacre, of the mob violence in the street, of returning to the Diamond J with Mary Ralston, and of Ellen Jenner's ultimatum.

"Go ahead."

He recounted riding out and meeting Peters and his men, and the hanging of Boone Ralston. As he spoke his eyes came around to look at Mary Ralston. She sat staring straight ahead, her small hands clasped tightly on the table before her.

"You saw them hang him?"

"No, but I found his body within minutes of the time. There's no doubt who murdered that boy."

A swell of voices rose through the courtroom.

Rudd sounded incredulous. "And you did nothing about it?"

"I have warrants for the arrest of Peters and Stover in my pocket. I was prevented from serving them last night." He stared fixedly at the Colonel. "I mean to serve them as soon as I leave this stand."

The noise in the courtroom became a clamor. Peters got to his feet, pivoted and started for the door. The judge spoke sharply to the sheriff.

"Stop that man."

The sheriff jumped in surprise. He turned his head and stared after Peters, but he made no move to follow. Box P men who had been scattered among the spectators came to their feet and, as if daring anyone to interfere, swaggered toward the entrance.

The judge watched them in helpless anger, but not until the last one had vanished through the doorway did he grasp his gavel and pound upon the desk.

"Quiet, quiet, or I'll have the courtroom cleared."

It took several minutes for the noise to subside, and when it did the judge glared out over his spectacles at the jury.

"I am stopping this trial," he said. "The prosecution has failed to establish a case against Mary Ralston, and the three witnesses produced by the state are obviously prejudiced and so involved in the happenings that their testimony is, in my opinion, valueless. You are thereby instructed, without leaving the box, to return a verdict of not guilty."

They gawped back at him.

"You heard me."

Slowly they nodded. Slowly the foreman looked down the line of the panel for confirmation. Then he again faced the judge.

"Your Honor, we find the defendant not guilty because of faulty evidence."

Laughter ran through the room, and a smile tugged at the corner of the judge's thin mouth. "All right, Frank. That's as good a reason as any. The defendant is dismissed. Court is adjourned. The sheriff is instructed to retain Al Craig, Haynes and Miss Ellen Jenner in custody. He is also instructed to arrest Colonel Peters and Dred Stover for the murder of Boone Ralston."

"I won't do it." The sheriff was on his feet, thumping the arm of his chair angrily. "You lost your mind, Thorne? They've got fifteen men out on that street and in their present mood they'll shoot anyone who steps through this door."

The judge peered down at him. "Meaning you're turning in your badge?"

The sheriff's mouth worked. Slowly he reached up and unfastened the star from his shirt pocket. "Take it." He threw it toward the judge's desk. It struck the edge, fell to the floor and lay almost at Jim Sanderson's feet.

The judge met Sanderson's eyes. "Well?"

Sanderson said, "I'll get them." He looked very tall, standing on the raised level of the witness box.

"I hereby appoint you a special officer of this court. Raise your right hand."

Thorne swore him in, and Sanderson left the box. The spectators stayed in their seats. Even the sheriff stood fast.

As Sanderson passed the counsel table Mary Ralston stood up suddenly. "Don't do it." Her voice was so low pitched that he barely heard the words. "Don't. They'll only kill you too. I couldn't stand that."

It sent a warmth racing through him. He smiled at her and began his long walk down the center aisle toward the outside door. He heard the crowd breaking up behind him. Men were moving to the side windows and dropping through them to the ground beyond. Short of the door he turned. Craig and Haynes were on their feet. Sanderson's eyes met those of the late sheriff.

"Keep hold of Craig. I'll kill you if he gets away."

He swung back then and went on toward the door, knowing that some of the curious had moved into the aisle behind him.

Three stone steps led down to the board

sidewalk. Sanderson stopped on the center step, looking across the empty hitch-rack at the men on the far side of the street. They had fanned out in a half circle. He did not count them, but he supposed there were fifteen, as Gilpen had said.

It was strange, he thought, standing thus in a town he had hardly heard of, facing men whom he had never known until a few days before, standing there, waiting for death.

Why should he be standing there? What was he trying to prove? He did not doubt his ability to kill Peters and Stover. He saw them in the middle of the semicircle, watching him. But there were too many other guns facing him, too great odds. Someone's gun held a bullet that would find him. Perhaps several guns.

He sent his challenge across the width of the dusty roadway. "All right, Colonel. I have a warrant for you, and one for Stover. Stand forward or I'll come and get you."

A laugh rose on the opposite boardwalk, a jeer which echoed from the false fronts of the sun warped buildings.

"Come and get us."

He came down to the bottom step, and then someone caught him from behind, arms about him, locking his own to his sides, and Ellen Jenner's voice sounded shrill and desperate in his ear.

"I've got him, Colonel, got him. Come running."

Sanderson's reaction was entirely instinctive. He threw himself forward. He might have broken the girl's hold, but that took time, and he had no time. Even as he fell he heard the hammer of guns from across the way, and heard Ellen Jenner scream.

He fell on his face, across the wooden walk, under the rail. Somewhere in the fall the girl had relaxed her grip. Now she lay across his legs. He did not try to get up. Miraculously, he had not been hit, although the bullets were splintering the boards around him, digging into the walls of the courthouse at his back.

He reached around and found his gun still in its holster. He drew it and sighted with calm deliberation on the Colonel, who had run to the center of the street to stop and stand firing steadily.

His first bullet caught Peters just under the heart and knocked him backward into the dust. The second struck Stover in the head. He turned his sights on the next man.

Behind him from the courthouse doorway another gun began to hammer, and he heard the judge's high, excited voice. "Get them, boy. Get them."

He squeezed off his next shot and suddenly something slammed him in the shoulder with the force of a sledge hammer. He transferred his gun to his left hand and knocked another man down, then he was hit again, this time in the back, and for an instant he could not move.

Then he saw that the men across the street, those still standing, had turned and were running toward the livery. He did not even fire after them. He heard the judge's gun, and then he heard the judge's voice again.

"How bad are you hit, boy?" Someone laid a hand on his shattered shoulder. He screamed under the sudden pain. Afterward he blacked out.

Eighteen

Three days later he roused, and the first person he saw was Mary Ralston, sitting beside the bed. Three weeks passed before he could sit up, and every day she was there, helping the doctor care for him. At the end of two months he was on his feet, his shoulder healing slowly.

"It will always be stiff," the doctor said. "But you're lucky. Luckier than most."

Peters was dead. Stover was dead, and Ellen Jenner had been killed in the street at his side.

Craig was still in jail. The judge had sent for extradition papers from Denver, and they had come through. It was morning, and Sanderson meant to ride that day. He sat in the lobby of the hotel and watched Mary Ralston slowly descend the stairs and rose to meet her.

"I'm leaving, you know."

She inclined her head.

"Mary." His right arm was still bandaged, still nearly useless. He laid his left hand on her arm. "Come with me."

She looked up at him, and suddenly there were tears in her eyes. "I can't, Jim."

"Why not?"

She said steadily, "I'd meant to. Even last night I meant to, but I can't. Every time I see you I think of Boone. Oh, it wasn't your fault, what happened. It was his own, but — but —"

"But if I'd taken him out of the valley as I promised it wouldn't have occurred."

"We'll never know."

He slipped his good arm about her and drew her to him, and surprisingly she lifted her mouth for his kiss. Then she pushed him away.

"That was for goodbye."

He stared at her a long moment, then turned and walked wordlessly from the lobby. He had almost reached the courthouse. Then he heard the sound of her boots, running on the sidewalk behind him. He turned and she came against him, panting a little from the run.

"Jim, Jim, I can't let you go alone. I can't. I can't."

He kissed her again. Suddenly the lifeless, drugged feeling which had filled him was swept away. He was about to kiss her another time when a voice called from the courthouse step and they turned to see Bryant Thorne staring down at them owlishly.

"You'd better come in here. A man who tries to be as legal as you can't go riding around the country with an unwed girl. Bring her inside while I get my book."